# GRIMSWORLD TALES

## DAVID HANKINS

Lost Bard Enterprises

EBook ISBN: 978-1-962740-08-1
Trade Paperback ISBN: 978-1-962740-06-7
Dust Jacket Hardcover ISBN: 978-1-962740-07-4

First Printing – December 2024

Cover design by Sarah Morrison

Published by
Lost Bard Enterprises LLC
PO Box 32
Bettendorf, IA 52722
david@davidhankins.com

# Also by David Hankins

## Grimsworld

*Death and the Taxman*
*Death and the Dragon*
*Death and the Immortal*
(Coming 2026)

*Grimsworld Tales*
(Companion Collection)

These books and more available at
www.davidhankins.com

To Beatrix, the inspiration behind my first short story.

To Michelle, thank you for such a fearsome daughter.

To any tax auditors reading this: Yes, I filed everything.
Why do you keep asking?

# CONTENTS

# About Grimsworld

*Grimsworld Tales* is a collection of short stories set in the same world as the novel *Death and the Taxman* and subsequent novels in the Grimsworld series. You might notice that the first short story "Death and the Taxman" has the same name as the novel, which is, I'll admit, confusing. After that short story won Writers of the Future, I expanded it into the full-length novel which published (of course) on Tax Day in 2024. The short story is included here to give a taste of Grimsworld to new readers, and to give fans of the novel a look at where it all began. As a bit of editorial slight of hand, you can tell the difference when I mention them because short stories have "Quotation Marks" and novels are *Italicized*.

Within these pages you'll find a lighthearted collection of stories. Tales to make you laugh, to make you cry, and perhaps to make you take up arms against a sea of troubles. And by opposing, end them.

To die—to sleep, no more.

Wait, that's *Hamlet*. My bad.

*Grimsworld Tales* centers around Death, the Grim Reaper, terror of men's souls. You know the guy: shiny skull, scythe, likes wearing black. Grim often finds himself surrounded by unlikely allies and terrifying foes. These are their stories. The origins of those whom Death would call his friends. Those who would stand by his side against enemies hellbent on stopping Grim in his endless quest to shepherd humanity's souls.

## Welcome to Grimsworld

# DEATH AND THE TAXMAN

## THE ORIGINAL SHORT STORY

I, THE GRIM REAPER, terror of men's souls, shall forevermore despise Mondays because that was the day I met Frank Totmann. That was the day I *became* Frank Totmann.

I found him having a heart attack in his dingy office on the third floor of the Colorado Springs Internal Revenue Service Tax Assistance Center. What a mouthful. They should have named it "The Land of Evil Auditors." Frank was a balding pudgy man without a single sharp edge. His cheap suit strained its buttons.

I stopped time and Frank gasped, clutching his chest and drawing relieved breaths. I pointed a bony finger, let my eye sockets flame a bit for effect, and intoned, "Frank Totmann, your time has come."

Frank sat back, threw me a broad smile, and said, "Cup of tea?" He produced a thermos and two teacups from under the desk.

How touching. Nobody ever offered refreshments. It's a lonely half-life, being Death, so I enjoy sharing folks' final moments. They usually complain about being too young to die or attempt to cheat me, but I don't mind. They're the only conversations I have. I nodded with gravity and grace.

What a fool I was. Never accept tea from a dying auditor.

I took a sip and coughed. It tasted of blood and ashes. Abrupt pain seared my bones, dropping me to my knees. The world spun, went dark, and with a distressing stretch which ended in a *pop,* I found myself sitting in Frank's chair staring across the desk at … me.

I blinked, shocked to have eyelids, and blinked again. No, that wasn't me. Frank Totmann's spirit, a mirror image of the body I now possessed, grinned stupidly in

Death's cowl. In *my* cowl, clutching *my* scythe—crafted by the Devil and blessed by the Almighty. It gave me power over human souls.

Of all the *cheek.*

I lunged across the desk, caught my hip on its edge, and sprawled across audit reports and tax returns. Breath whooshed out of me. Unfamiliar with a human body, I forgot to breathe in. Stars flashed before my eyes.

Frank jumped back, holding my scythe high like a bully taunting a child. I flopped onto his chair, which rolled back with plastic protests. I sucked in a breath, time resumed, and my heart pounded in my chest. Frank's chest. Whatever.

I grabbed the spilled teacup and sniffed it. It smelled of anise, copper, and ... *magic.* My eyes went wide. "How?" I asked, then flinched. The Grim Reaper should boom and intone, not squeak like a scared bureaucrat.

Frank's grin became a smirk. "Ancient soul transfer spell. Sumerian, I think. Doc said my heart was failing, so I nailed the timing of your arrival by taking poison. We shared the transference potion and voilà"—he took a bow—"I cheated Death."

I flung the teacup at the wall. It shattered and fell to the industrial carpet. How the hell had an IRS auditor unearthed a Sumerian soul transfer spell?

How dare he use it on *me*? On *Death*?

And after offering hospitality. Never again! Never again would I...

My mouth opened and closed like a dying fish as the gravity of the situation hit home.

Never again was right. I was a human. A flesh and blood human. Mortal.

More importantly, I was a mortal who—I checked my internal clock which measured human lives—should have died five minutes ago. My gaze flicked to Frank. To the scythe in his hands.

He followed my gaze and shook his head. "I'm not reaping your soul. Not even sure how, to tell the truth. But"—he twirled my scythe then swung it like a golf club—"I'll get the hang of it. Besides, that body's not dead. I spiked my tea with the poison's antidote." He waggled his fingers at me, said "See ya!" and drifted through the door.

I slouched in the chair, dumbfounded for the first time in millennia. The Rules were quite clear. Frank's soul was supposed to cross over today. I had to swap us back, restore the balance before Hell's bureaucrats noticed. Before Hell's Auditor noticed and took *my* soul instead.

***

I sat in Frank's office for an hour, my mind chasing its tail. How do I, the Grim Reaper, cheat death? This heart may have resumed beating, but it couldn't last long. My hands, used to clutching my scythe, grasped at the air. I grabbed a pen and clicked it obsessively.

It wasn't the same.

A knock at the door interrupted my thoughts and a short, solid woman with pinned-back, graying hair swung the door open. She wore a matronly flowered dress, an overabundance of clattering jewelry, and a smile that lit her face like she was genuinely pleased to see me.

That was a new experience.

"Staying late, Frank?" Her voice was warm, like honey.

I clicked the pen a few more times and read her soul through her dark brown eyes. Cordelia Knowles, fifty-eight years old, death in forty-three years. "Uh, no," I said and rose awkwardly.

"Walk me to my car?"

"Sure, uh, Cordelia."

Her brows knit together. "It's Cora. I told you on our first date." Her voice slowed, and she tilted her head. "You okay, Frank? You look like death warmed over."

*You have no idea.* Aloud I tried to say "I'm fine," but the words stuck in my throat. I grimaced. Bloody Archangel Gabriel and his bloody restrictions. He'd burned the words "Honesty in Death" into my soul when he made me the Reaper.

I couldn't lie.

An agent of both Heaven and Hell must remain above reproach. It was one of Heaven's Rules that governed all spiritual matters. I'd never chafed under that restriction before today.

After flapping my jowls again like that bloody dying fish, I said, "I'm alive. That's what's important." I stomped around the desk and followed Cora into a cubicle farm with people streaming toward an elevator. She gave me a piercing look but didn't press. Instead, she chattered about work and my thoughts turned inward.

Frank had found a Sumerian spell. There had to be a reversal. I nodded to myself. Yes, that was the ticket. Find

Frank's house, retrieve his spell book, and get out of this body.

My thoughts were again interrupted when Cora looped her arm in mine and guided me around the crowd to a door marked EXIT. I reached it first and tried to pass through.

Like I always do.

My face smacked into solid wood, and I bounced off, popping the door open. I stumbled back, hands flying to my nose. "Ow!"

The departing crowd burst into laughter with a smattering of applause. Someone called, "Been walking long, Frank?"

"No," I said, rubbing my nose and glaring at the offending door as it swung back toward me. The laws of physics were so ... inconvenient. Cora placed a comforting hand on my shoulder, and we pushed into the stairwell.

"Frank? Are you sure you're okay?"

I patted her hand noncommittally and headed downstairs. At the bottom, I was careful to press on the push bar before stepping outside. I felt inordinately pleased with myself when it worked.

Bright sunlight made me blink. The city of Colorado Springs rose on foothills, climbing partway up an imposing ridgeline. The cool wind was crisp and plucked at my suit. I drew a deep, invigorating breath. I drew another, feeling alive in a way I'd never known. Cora hooked my elbow again and guided me toward her rusty Peugeot. I recognized the car because I'd reaped a soul from one last week. In midair. It had blown through an Alpine guardrail to plummet off a cliff. The deceased had blamed the car for his demise, never mind the half-written text on his cell phone.

"Well, this is me," Cora said, fishing keys from her purse. "Are we still on for tonight?"

"To ... night?"

"Yes, silly. Dinner? At Edelweiss? You said you'd never tried schnitzel."

"I have not tried schnitzel." I spoke with finality, reveling in an easy truth.

She gave me a bemused smile, opened her door, then paused as if waiting. Her brown eyes locked with mine then, to my horror, she rocked forward and pecked me on the lips. Blood rushed to Cora's cheeks, and she slid into her car. "See you at seven!" She waved and was gone. I stood there, dumbfounded for the second time.

She'd kissed me. I ... I'd never been kissed. It felt odd, this mashing of body parts together, and it left my lips feeling tingly. Perhaps it was the wind. Yes, that was it.

I gave myself a shake. Find Frank, reverse the spell. Stay focused on what mattered before the Auditor found out. Hell's final arbiter of the Rules would love to banish me to the Realm of Torments. Forever.

I headed for the nearest road to find a cab. I'd reaped too many souls from crumpled wrecks to try driving. Traffic flowed past in a noisy blur until I waved down a taxi. I carefully opened the car door as Cora had done.

Success. I was getting the hang of this human thing.

"Where to, pal?" the cabbie asked. I automatically checked his soul through his cheerful gray eyes. Louis Faretti, thirty-six, death in seven years.

"The home of Frank Totmann, Louis," I said, sliding inside. The cab smelled of industrial cleaners and artificial lemon with a whiff of vomit. Louis hung one arm over the bench seat.

"Got an address, bud?" I blinked at him then rummaged through Frank's pockets. Wallet, keys, cell phone. I dug into the wallet, found something with Frank's picture and address, and read it aloud. Louis nodded and sped away, tires screeching. Horns blared as we wove violently through traffic.

Over the next six minutes of terror, I discovered why the cab smelled of vomit. I managed, barely, to keep my gorge down as Louis chatted.

"Whatcha do for a living?"

"For the living, nothing. The dead are my concern." I clutched the door as we zoomed around a truck.

"Coroner? Huh. Never drove a coroner before." He glanced in his rearview. "You're looking kinda pale, bud. Rough day at the office? Someone send you a body that wasn't quite dead yet?" He chuckled and slammed on the brakes as traffic stopped around us. I rocked forward and caught myself on his seat.

"Uh, yes," I said, falling back as the cab shot forward and resumed weaving through traffic. "He stole something very valuable." *My identity as Death.* "Failure to retrieve it will have dire consequences." Eternal torments. I shuddered.

Louis's eyes went wide. "A real Lazarus story, but with a twist. Ain't that wild? So, what, you gonna get fired?" Someone honked as Louis cut them off. We passed into the ridgeline's shadow and the temperature dropped.

I glowered at the back of his head. Lazarus was a fluke. Divine intervention which ruined my perfect record and nearly led to an audit.

"Worse," I said. "I could face Judgment." Judgment long delayed for my original sin. My mind shied away from that train of thought.

We screeched to a stop before a sad-looking house with cracked tan siding and brown grass. "That'll be twelve bucks even," Louis said.

I blinked at him, then remembered. Money. Humans used money for everything. I handed him Frank's wallet.

Louis arched an eyebrow and retrieved some bills before handing it back. He passed me a card. "If you need a ride, give me a ring." His head cocked to one side. "Never caught your name, friend."

"Grim Reaper." I fumbled at the door handle, which was different from the one outside the car.

Louis barked a laugh as the door popped open and I tumbled out. "Man, your parents had a twisted sense of humor. No wonder you became a coroner. See ya, Grim!" He waved and sped off. I set my jaw and approached Frank's house.

Getting inside proved challenging. Why was *every* door handle different? This one had a stupid little knob that wouldn't turn.

*Keys, right.*

The door creaked open, releasing an overwhelming stench of old coffee and stale sweat. Piles of clutter lay everywhere. I wrinkled my nose. Why did humans cling to life so tenaciously when *this* was how they lived?

I searched the main floor but found little of interest beyond a bookshelf overflowing with occult and religious texts. I scanned the titles. Plenty about the afterlife and Yours Truly, but nothing ancient. No Sumerian soul spells, just an unhealthy fascination with death.

No surprise there.

I paused at a bulletin board tacked with thank you notes from clients Frank had audited, gratitude for helping clear debt and acquire refunds. Odd. I wouldn't have expected such helpful behavior from an auditor.

From his kitchen, I descended a stairwell to the center of an unfinished basement. Creaky steps echoed through darkness before my hand brushed against a light switch. A bulb flickered on, revealing the logical result of Frank's occult research. Painted archaic symbols covered the empty cement floor, each with unlit candles at intersection points. Summoning circles from different civilizations.

Bingo.

I recognized Babylonian, Greek, Chinese, Egyptian, and—ah-ha!—Sumerian. That one had intricately woven runes surrounding charred cement and feathery ash.

I circled the dank room, stepping around the summoning circles, examining each. It was a testament to mankind's tenacity that every civilization devised methods of controlling spirits. Tucked under the open stairs was Frank's workspace—a tattered recliner beside a rickety apothecary cabinet filled with papers, moldering books, and scrolls. Artifacts in labeled jars and little plastic baggies hid in the apothecary cabinet's little cubbyholes. Stickers decorated many with RARE FIND!—CORDELIA'S APOTHECARY SUPPLY.

I arched an eyebrow. Cordelia? She was a tax auditor *and* an apothecary? Interesting.

I retrieved a rolled-up bundle of copy paper. Pictures of ancient Sumerian tablets filled every page with handwritten translations scrawled along the edges. My breath caught and the papers crinkled in my grip. This was it.

I drew a deep breath, smoothed out the papers, and read. I wasn't limited by human language barriers, so translation wasn't a problem.

The content was.

There was nothing here about swapping souls. It was a simple summoning spell.

I dropped into the recliner with a huff and read through again. Nothing. I scratched my jaw.

Perhaps Frank summoned a spirit and got the spell from them. I eyed the apothecary cabinet's little cubbyholes. Follow Frank's steps. Summon a demon, then ask it about the spell. I nodded to myself, jumped up, and set to work.

Fifteen minutes later the Sumerian circle was set up with candles, cinnamon, and bone dust from a Sumerian priest—if the baggie label was to be believed. I turned off the light, chanted the incantation seven times, then pricked my finger over the circle before snatching my hand back.

A bolt of red lightning arced up when my blood hit the cement. It bounced off the circle's invisible walls, splitting and multiplying until an inferno of crackling red electricity connected cement to bare joists. My skin tingled and my hair stood on end before the entire light show condensed into a single bolt again. It struck the center of the circle with a hellish boom that rattled the stairs. Lava bubbled through the cement and from that rose a demon's hideous form, clad in a wrinkled gray suit.

He stood only two feet tall.

I smiled, the knot in my chest easing somewhat. It was Alvin, recently promoted head of Bureaucratic Torments. Not a friend, really, but our paths had crossed. Horns poked through his thin, greasy comb-over and his sharp red eyes glared at me. He pointed a clawed finger.

"That's it, Frank! I'm sending my cousin Brutus to make your life a living hell until the *day … you … die*! Then, when your soul finds its way to Hell, I'm gonna—"

"I am not Frank Totmann," I said, and Alvin paused, his angry glower turning to confusion. He focused on my eyes then gasped.

"In the name of Lucifer," he whispered, "he did it." Alvin's brows scrunched. "Oh, Grim. How you doing?"

Heat surged through my chest and my breath came short and fast. "You … you knew?" I stepped forward, fists clenched, breaking the circle with a flash of red electricity. "You *knew* Frank Totmann's plan and didn't *think* to warn me? He stole my scythe! My power! My very identity!" My hand shot toward Alvin's throat, but he leapt back.

"It wasn't like that!" His hands flew up, warding me off as I stalked forward. "Frank's daily summonings were annoying the crap out of me. I had to give him something, so I found a soul transfer spell he couldn't use. The ingredients were impossible to acquire." Alvin slid under the open stairs between the recliner and apothecary cabinet.

"Impossible? Look at me! I'm stuck in a human body"—I slapped the stairs for emphasis as I ducked under—"thanks to *you*!"

Alvin flinched and dodged back around the Egyptian circle. "The spell required the bones of a Sumerian priest!"

"You idiot!" I spun toward the cabinet, snatched a labeled baggie, and read it aloud, "Sumerian Priest Bone Dust." I threw the bag at Alvin, and it passed through his chest and slid across the floor. "That was a basic ingredient of his summoning circle!"

Alvin held a finger up to protest, but his words died unspoken. His finger lowered slowly. "Oh. Uh, sorry."

My anger flared hot before draining away. I sat heavily on the stairs and dropped my head into my hands. "Me too. More than you could possibly imagine." I drew a shuddering breath then looked up. "Was there a reversal on that Sumerian spell?"

"How should I know?" Alvin's flippancy brought me to my feet, fists clenched again. He raised placating hands. "But I can check."

I drew deep, calming breaths. Death was supposed to be emotionless, impartial. The first time I got angry, *really* angry, had been over something stupid. An argument with the Auditor about sins and sacrifices. I'd been an angel then. So young. I'd tried to prove my point, whispered a lie into Cain's ear, and accidentally incited him to murder Abel.

Humanity's first death. Their first murder. Heaven had still been reeling with the aftershocks of Lucifer's betrayal and dropped me into Purgatory to await Judgment. To avoid eternal torment, I begged Gabriel for clemency. I could atone for my crime by easing mankind's souls into the next world.

He bought it and I sidestepped Judgment, which really pissed off the Auditor. He'd been angling for the job.

Thus was the Grim Reaper born. No longer an angel, not quite a demon, bound to serve both Heaven and Hell and beholden to neither.

My pocket vibrated with a cheerful chirp, and I jumped. I dug out Frank's phone and read the message on the screen.

Cora: *I'm at Edelweiss! You on your way?*

Alvin stepped around to peer at the screen. "You old dog," he said, turning corporeal and punching my shoulder. "One day as a human, and you've already got a date!"

I rose, shielding the phone from his view. "Frank had dinner plans before he died. Well, almost died. There is no need to maintain his schedule." My stomach twitched with unfamiliar pain and gurgled.

Alvin looked at my belly, then the phone, and chuckled. "You're human now, subject to four incessant needs."

I raised an imperious eyebrow at the dirty-minded cretin. "Implying what?"

Alvin barked a laugh. "No, Grim, not sex. That's necessary for species survival, not the individual. No, you'll need an appalling amount of food, water, and sleep to keep that body functional." He made a shooing gesture. "Go. Go on your date. I'll see what I can find about reversing that spell."

I nodded and said, "Thank you." Cora might also provide insights since she'd provided the ingredients.

Alvin gave a double thumbs-up and sank through the floor without the dramatic flair of his entrance.

"Wait!" I called. "You said humans have four needs. Hunger, thirst, sleep, and...?"

Alvin's descent paused at neck level and his face split into a broad smile. "Pooping, my friend. What goes in, must come out. A serious design flaw, if you ask me. Good luck!" He waved cheerfully and disappeared.

My breath whooshed out and I dropped back onto the stairs, making them groan. I often reaped souls from compromising positions, so I had a vague idea of what was coming, but I had never considered the mechanics of ... defecation. My mind skittered around, refusing to focus. My gut rumbled, and I realized that I was, indeed, hungry.

Well, best get on with it. I retrieved Frank's cell phone.

***

I stumbled from Louis's cab with shaky knees after he screeched to a halt outside Edelweiss restaurant. "Enjoy dinner!" he called, then zoomed away.

Low lights shone inside the stone-faced farmhouse and the hum of conversation drifted from outdoor seating to the left. Dishes clanked and propane heaters glowed red as jacketed diners enjoyed fall's dying warmth. I shivered in Frank's thin suit, hoping Cora's table was inside. I headed for the door.

Sharp pain sliced through my chest, arcing into my left shoulder. I gasped and dropped onto a bench. Frank's heart gave four syncopated beats before settling down again. I drew a deep breath and massaged my chest. This heart was past its expiration date. It wouldn't last much longer.

A young man inside escorted me to a corner booth in a room topped with faux roof eaves. Blue and white checkered bunting, a cloud-painted ceiling, and rough wooden panels gave the impression of outdoor dining without the chill Colorado winds. Cora beamed when she saw me.

"Hey, there. I was worried you'd stand me up."

"I apologize for my tardiness. I usually make a point of arriving just when people need me." What would happen to a soul if I didn't arrive on time? Would the body die and decay with the soul trapped inside? Would that be my fate? Disturbed by my thoughts, I slid into the booth.

Cora said, "I ordered for us. You're going to *love* the Jägerschnitzel."

As if on cue, a waiter arrived with plates. I eyed mine with trepidation. Everything was a uniform brown. Breaded meat was buried under thick mushroom gravy, and piled french fries threatened to topple off the plate. The fries were sprinkled with a red powder which added a spicy kick to the greasy scents wafting upward.

It smelled fantastic. My stomach agreed with loud gurgles.

I glanced at Cora, but she had already dug in. New to the intricacies of eating, I copied what she did. The silverware was tricky, but I managed my first bite.

Greasy bliss melted on my tongue. I closed my eyes and a groan escaped as I chewed and swallowed.

"See, told you it was good."

I gazed into Cora's smiling eyes. "That was ... amazing." I cut another bite. "Is all food this good?" No wonder humans spent so much of their lives eating. That bite followed the first and I groaned again as she nodded.

"Here? Most of it. If you have room for dessert, their Apfelstrudel is to die for."

"To die for?" A third and fourth bite disappeared. "I'll take the chance."

Cora chuckled, a warm sound that revealed her bright soul.

Dinner passed in a blur. The waiter brought us beers that looked like bubbly swamp water. I took one sip and gagged. It tasted like swamp water too. Cora seemed content to talk about herself, her grown kids, and her dreams for the future while I ate. Turned out that she dreamed of expanding her online apothecary supply shop.

"Where do you acquire your artifacts?" I asked.

"That's the joy of the internet. You can find anything if you dig hard enough."

*Like a soul-swapping spell reversal?*

The waiter derailed my line of questioning with a fluffy pastry that oozed baked apples and cinnamon. Pillowy vanilla ice cream lay atop the Apfelstrudel, melting in thin streams. It smelled divine.

I took a large bite and Cora asked, "So what are your dreams?"

"Hmmph?" I mumbled around the glorious blending of hot, cold, and sweet.

"Nobody wants to be a tax auditor when they grow up. What else do you want?"

I swallowed and sat back. What did *I* want? Nobody had asked me that before. I searched my soul. "I like my job, helping souls in need. I'm good at it, but it gets lonely."

Cora gripped my hand, her bracelets jangling. "You're not alone anymore. Did you know that the girls at the office tried to warn me off? Said that a confirmed bachelor must have deep, dark secrets." She released my hand, leaving a ghost of warmth on my skin. "I'm glad I didn't listen. You're really quite sweet."

"Awww…," said a voice from under the table. "Too bad you'll have to break her heart." Alvin's pinched face poked above the table as he climbed onto the bench beside Cora. "Time to leave, Grim. Now!"

"Why?" I said. "What did you find?"

Cora followed my gaze to the empty seat—humans can't see spirits who didn't want to be seen—and creased her brows.

"No time, lover boy," Alvin said. "Hell has noticed your absence. The Auditor is coming."

His words were a punch in the gut. "How'd he find out so fast, Alvin?"

Cora's eyebrows shot up. "Alvin? The demon?" Frank must have told her about the summonings. She scooted into the booth's corner and dug an iron cross from her purse.

Alvin gave the artifact a dismissive nose wrinkle and ran a clawed hand through his greasy hair. "There's a worldwide epidemic of miraculous survivals and recoveries. Your replacement isn't doing his job. Nobody could find you, so they've sent the Auditor to clean up." Alvin glanced anxiously over his shoulder then swore.

I followed his gaze and jumped in my seat. "Damn!" Diners glanced up, but they couldn't see what I saw. A massive demon ducked into the restaurant. He was impossibly gaunt, like stretched dough, and wore a rumpled suit that matched Alvin's. Gold-rimmed spectacles covered blood-red eyes which scanned the room. Claws drummed on the back of an oversized clipboard.

"Frank?" Cora sounded scared as she grabbed my hand and swung the cross to follow my gaze. "What's wrong?"

"Death comes for all men," I whispered, a shiver running through me.

The Auditor saw me and made a check on his clipboard. "Frank Totmann," he said in a voice as dry as crumpled ash. "Your time is past." He lumbered forward, one arm outstretched. He didn't have a scythe to snip my soul's tether with this body, but he could rip it out and drag me to Hell with him.

Fear turned schnitzel to lead in my stomach. You can't run from Death. I would know.

I glanced at the clipboard, eyes narrowed. He wasn't Death. He was the Auditor. You can evade the Auditor, for a while at least.

I squeezed Cora's hand. "He cannot touch you. Your time is not yet come." Her wide eyes bulged as I pulled myself free and bolted for the exit.

***

Evading the Auditor was simple, yet terribly difficult. I had to abandon every resource Frank had. The lumbering demon gave chase, but his skills lay in tracking through files and records, not in active pursuit. I lost him after a few heart-wrenching hours by squeezing behind a strip mall dumpster.

I had nowhere to go. I had to avoid Frank's house. His office. Cora. The Auditor could track me through her. Ditching Frank's phone when she called had felt like cutting off my arm. Any information she had about Frank's spell was now lost.

I woke with a start the following morning. I'd been having a nightmare of fleeing the Auditor through a maze of doors, each with its own bloody different handle. My heartbeat slowed. Orange-dappled clouds drifted past, visible through the gap between dumpster and building. I hadn't felt sleep sneak up as the temperature dropped.

I squeezed out of my hiding place and into a parking lot, stamping warmth into my tingling toes. My joints protested, cold muscles so tight that I could barely walk. I shielded my eyes against the low sun. I didn't know where I was.

An unfamiliar pressure on my bowels made me grimace. Alvin's fourth incessant need had found me. I trudged across the parking lot toward a gas station. A bell tinkled as I entered and warm air washed over me, inducing a wave of relaxation. Heavens, that felt good.

The pressure on my bowels intensified.

"Toilet?" I asked the lanky teen behind the counter. He pointed to the back without looking up from his phone. I followed his vague directions, found the toilet, and discovered the heinous reality of defecation. Mortality's dark side.

Humans do this every day? I would rather die.

I flushed, scrubbed my hands as if cleaning the stain off my soul, and fled the restroom.

The bell chimed again as I left the gas station. I huddled against the wind and stopped, not sure where to go next.

"Grim?"

I jumped and looked toward the voice, ready to run. Louis waved from behind a car he was fueling. Not his cab, but a beat-up green sedan.

"Brother, you look awful," he said. "Date didn't go well?"

I shrugged. "Dinner was amazing. Cora was charming. But then ... he found me."

"The guy who stole from you?"

I shook my head. "No. A Hell-spawned demon called the Auditor. He ... you wouldn't understand."

Louis stepped around his car, concern in his gray eyes. "I understand the look of a man running from his mistakes. Everything looks bad when you're in the middle of it." He held out a hand. "Come on, let me take you to breakfast.

You'll see things clearer with a full stomach and some caffeine."

My stomach rumbled. "Thank you. Your generosity is—"

An iron vice seized my chest and my breath wheezed out. I dropped to the pavement, struggling for air, muscles turning watery. Frank's traitorous heart seized again, sending a spike through the vice.

"Grim!" Louis knelt beside me, a hand on my back. "What's wrong?"

"Heart ... attack. Third in ... two days."

"Hey!" he yelled at the kid inside. "Give me a hand!"

I grabbed his arm. "Please ... don't let me die." My heart beat rapidly to make up for lost time, taunting me with hope.

"Hold on, Grim. You're not dying today."

I collapsed. Rough pavement scratched my face, and my brain turned fuzzy. Strong arms lifted me into Louis's back seat. The door slammed, the engine started, and we tore out of the lot.

The world became snapshots of consciousness as Louis wove through traffic, blaring his horn. Anxious assurances washed over me while I struggled to survive. To live. Finding Frank was a distant desire. Avoiding the Auditor more immediate. Would he recognize my soul as he ripped it out? Would it make a difference to my fate?

"No hospital," I wheezed, but Louis didn't hear me. A hospital would put Frank's name on record. The Auditor would see it.

We screeched to a stop, Louis yelled for help, and more hands pulled me from the car.

"What happened?" a woman asked in a no-nonsense tone as they laid me on a gurney.

"Heart attack. Third in two days," Louis said.

"And he's still *breathing*? Death's not ready for this guy. What's his name?"

"Grim Reaper."

"*Not* the time for jokes." Her voice turned severe, and a hand dug into my pocket. "Says Frank Totmann on his license."

*No. Please.* I reached for the wallet, but my hand flopped uselessly. They wheeled me inside. Lights flashed past overhead as nurses rushed me ... somewhere. We pushed into a brightly lit room that smelled of antiseptic. Louis's anxious face peered through the windowed door, his lips moving with silent prayer.

Pain exploded in my chest, and I screamed. My eyes bulged and I squeezed a hand I found in mine.

"Crash cart, now!" the nurse yelled—

Time stopped so abruptly that I felt jolted out of reality.

The pain ... paused. The room's flurry of activity froze midmotion. I sagged, drawing ragged breaths.

Frank glided through the wall, smirking from the depths of my cowl, my scythe in hand. "Dying sucks, huh?" he said.

Cheeky, insufferable, little son of a...

I sat up, gauging the distance between us. "You toy with powers you don't understand, Frank Totmann."

"I'm figuring it out. The stopping time thing is pretty cool. Last night I played a round of golf with a dying CEO before sending him on his way." He twirled my scythe then pretended to putt.

"You are supposed to grant an opportunity for confession. Not ... play golf." I shook my head, appalled, and swiveled my legs off the table.

Frank swung the scythe back into a two-handed grip and ducked behind a nurse frozen in frantic motion. He glanced at the clock on the wall. "It's been a bit longer for me, what with stopping time, but I figured you'd have more than sixteen hours. How'd you like being human?"

"It was terrifying, confusing, and … enjoyable. I found your fellow humans thoughtful and kind. I had a date with Cora."

Frank's eyes went wide. "Ah, crap. I forgot about that. I meant to cancel."

"She helped you prepare. You didn't tell her your plan?"

He bit one lip and said, "I couldn't. Didn't want to see her cry. She's gonna be heartbroken when I die. Well, when you die."

"Everybody leaves loved ones behind. We all have unfinished business."

His grip tightened on the scythe, and he nodded, stepping back around the nurse. "Well, I guess it's time. Best of luck in the afterlife!" He pulled the scythe back, readying the Reaper's power over the soul.

Realization hit me like an avalanche, and my breath caught. I didn't need to reverse Frank's Sumerian spell. I needed my scythe. The Reaper's scythe didn't just sever souls from their mortal coil. It moved them to where they were supposed to be.

I was supposed to be in that cowl and Frank in this body.

I held up a hand. "Wait! You can't reap me."

Frank's eyes narrowed, my death over his shoulder, my salvation in his hands. "Why not?"

"The Auditor is coming for you."

Fear crept into Frank's voice. "The who?"

"The Auditor. Hell's final arbiter of the Rules. Hell noticed discrepancies after you took my place. The Auditor *hates* discrepancies and metes out punishment with ... finality." Frank lowered the scythe and glanced around furtively.

"I'm not taking my body back. I already cheated death."

*Yes, you were the first. I will be the second.*

I leaned forward conspiratorially. "Here's what we'll—"

The words froze in my throat as the Auditor lurched through the door. Claws scratched angry gouges on the back of his clipboard as he pointed it at me. "Frank Totmann, your time is past! I—"

He noticed the real Frank Totmann, and his brows bunched together behind gold-wire frames. "Two Frank Totmanns?" He consulted his clipboard. "This is highly irregular." He considered me, but I kept my eyes averted, hoping he wouldn't recognize my soul. Frank made the mistake of meeting his gaze.

Tension drained from the Auditor's shoulders. He straightened and adjusted his glasses. "There you are. Your Judgment is at hand." He eyed the scythe, then me. I saw connections click in his evil mind. A dark smile stole over his face. "You have failed, Grim. It's time to face *your* Judgment. It's time for a new Reaper." He turned to Frank. "I'll start with this impostor's soul."

Frank stumbled backward, lip quivering. "No!"

I jumped off the gurney. "Give me the scythe!"

"*No!*" Panic tainted Frank's words and the Auditor lunged at him. Frank leapt between two nurses and the Auditor followed, implacable. They danced around my gurney, just out of reach. I had to do something. Anything to keep the Auditor from my scythe.

"Wait!" I yelled and leapt between them, throwing my hands out like a referee separating boxers. Frank scrambled back, but the Auditor thrust a long-fingered hand into my chest. He gripped my soul.

Cold washed through me and I felt myself dying all over again. My breath wheezed. Frank's wide eyes met mine and I turned my palm up, beseeching.

"Please, before he drags us both into Hell with him."

Frank's gaze whipped to the Auditor who yanked at my soul, half tearing it from my body. I screamed and collapsed to my knees.

Frank shook his head.

"I'll ... make you an apprentice!"

"But..."

"Or you die!"

Frank quivered, then nodded and thrust the scythe into my hands.

Power flowed into me. Power to stop time and parse souls. Power over life itself. I smelled the cherry blossoms of Heaven and the burning sulfur of Hell, an intoxicating brew that overwhelmed my pain.

I spun on my knees to slam the scythe into the Auditor's chest, but he caught the handle with a *crack*. Lightning surged around his grip, and he tried to yank the scythe away.

He failed.

"You are not Death," I intoned. "You never will be."

I rose, scythe between us, and shed Frank Totmann's skin and cheap suit. They drifted away like flaming embers that pushed onto Frank's terrified soul, leaving me a proud, naked skeleton. The embers solidified and Frank became flesh once more. I shrouded my skeletal form in a cowled cloak of darkness drawn from Hell itself.

*I* was Death.

I kicked the Auditor in the chest and wrenched my scythe away. He flew through a frozen nurse and the wall with a furious roar. He'd be back.

I spun and pointed an accusing finger. "Frank Totmann, you cannot run from Death."

"Wait, what? No! You said…" He fell back and bumped into the crash cart, making the wheels squeak. I placed my blade to his throat and a sob escaped him. "Please, I don't want to die."

"I understand," I whispered, and I did. I really did. He squeezed his eyes shut and pressed back. I swung my scythe and reaped Frank's soul. His body collapsed, and his spirit bobbed into the ether beside me. I gripped his shoulder to keep him in place and turned as the Auditor stormed in.

"Frank Totmann is dead," I said. "The scales are balanced; the Rules are satisfied. You have nothing further to audit here."

He glanced at Frank's soul, then at my scythe. Raw desire and bitter realization burned in his red eyes. The Rules forbade interfering with Death's duties, and he was more bound to the Rules than I. The loophole created by Frank's spell had just closed. "Damn you." His fists clenched. "Where will you send him?"

"Not your concern."

The Auditor cursed and retrieved his clipboard. He made a definitive checkmark which sounded like it tore through parchment. "I'm watching you, Grim," he said, then stomped away through the wall.

I counted to twenty to ensure that he was gone before starting time again. A cacophony of noise and action burst into the room. The nurses scrambled, confused to find Frank's body beside the crash cart. One checked his vitals, sagged, then declared him dead.

Frank looked up as they carted his body away. "You killed me."

"No, your body died. I retrieved your soul. A minor, but important distinction."

"Now what? Were you serious about making me an apprentice?"

I rubbed my chin. "I could use the company. And you've proven quite resourceful. For a human."

He sighed, relief twitching the corners of his lips. "Alright, Boss, what first? Do I get my own scythe?"

I gave him a flaming stare. "First, we correct your errors from the past day. There are souls who need to pass on. For failing at your assumed duties, you must take their confessions."

"But I didn't know what I was doing!"

"That's no excuse. Every soul deserves your utmost care. Come, I will show you."

I held onto Frank and followed the incessant pull of a soul in need of transition.

***

I will forevermore hold a grudge against Mondays, for that was the traumatic day I became human. Yet, at the same time, I found my brief life surprisingly enjoyable.

Well, except for the dying.

And the defecation.

Tuesdays, however, will hold a special place in my heart. Tuesday brought me an apprentice, whom I hope will eventually become a friend.

Frank finished taking a recently deceased granny's confession and we proceeded to the next soul. He would need a new name. "Death and Frank" lacked the proper authoritative ring.

I snapped my bony fingers, remembering. Frank already had a title. One which sparked fear and caution among the living. Together we would shepherd souls to their final rest as the two greatest certainties in life.

Death and the Taxman.

*This, the original short story version of "Death and the Taxman" that won Writers of the Future (published in Writers of the Future Volume 39, May 2023), is generally the first four chapters of the novel of the same name. I'm sure the keen reader can note the differences, especially the point at which the short story became a novel with lots of new characters and some interesting new problems for Grim. If you haven't read the full length novel, consider this short story a mere taste of what is to come once you do.*

*"Death and the Taxman" was born as the writing community mourned the passing of Writers of the Future co-ordinating judge David Farland (Wolverton). Death is the ultimate rigged game, one that the Grim Reaper never loses. But what if he did? What if he became human? Would the Grim Reaper cling to life as tenaciously as we do?*

*I would argue that yes, yes he would. And while he would struggle to survive this craziness we call life, I think he would enjoy the little pleasures we take for granted. Like schnitzel and apfelstrudel.*

*"Death and the Taxman" was also named the Best Science Fiction and Fantasy Short Story of 2023 in the Critters Readers' Poll.*

# Hell's Bureaucracy

Knowledge wasn't power, it was a curse.

Sam knew he hadn't misfiled anything, let alone the Waters account Form-5, but here he was, once again, taking the blame. He rocked back on his heels under Mr. Langowski's tirade, wishing he could explain everything.

*Yes, sir. I did confirm receipt with accounting. Especially after last time.*

*No, files aren't in the habit of walking away. This one had help.*

*As a matter of fact, I do know who helped it walk away. It was the thieving little demon sitting on the cubicle wall right behind you.*

They'd toss him in the loony bin!

Alvin, the two-foot-tall miscreant that only Sam saw, cackled from his perch as the boss's tirade escalated. Spittle hit Sam's cheek, and he flinched.

What a way to start the week.

Langowski finally left, and Sam collapsed into his chair and glared at Alvin. What he wouldn't give to escape the little hellion's torments. The demon looked pleased with himself and straightened his rumpled gray suit. Scrawny horns poked through his greasy comb-over, and his sharp red eyes twinkled.

"So, how was your weekend?" Alvin's voice sounded like a strangled weasel.

"Fine. Should have known you'd put in overtime just to make my Monday morning special." Sam kept his voice low.

Alvin grinned. Even demons like getting credit for a job well done. "I foresee a new policy coming. Form-5s in quadruplicate!" Sam groaned. The Form-5 was Alvin's invention. The little imp had turned Bridewell Incorporated into his personal bureaucratic playground, implementing crazy policies that everyone accepted. People don't question bureaucracy, they just complain about it. Sam sold corporate office supplies for Bridewell, which sucked, but he didn't have any better options. He'd been sacked twice because of Alvin.

The phone rang and Sam answered. He listened to the shrill voice at the other end, saying "uh-huh" and "okay" as appropriate before hanging up. He eyed Alvin. "Why are there two pallets of neon pink copy paper downstairs with my name on the order slip?"

Alvin's smile broadened, and Sam rolled his eyes. He'd expected more physical torment from his personally assigned demon—hot pincers, haunted dreams, that sort of thing—but Alvin's torments were more insidious. Bureaucratic.

Sam drummed his fingers on the desk. Two pallets of pink paper. Langowski would blow a gasket. He heaved himself up and headed for the elevator.

The loading dock smelled of diesel fumes despite the open bay door that let in chill January winds. Alvin scurried away as Sam headed toward the receiving desk, and he breathed a sigh of relief. Good riddance.

A portly truck driver stepped from behind the double-stacked pallets of paper and Sam froze. It wasn't the driver who struck him speechless, but the hulking angel standing *behind* the man, a claymore on his back. The angel's bushy blonde eyebrows rose when he realized Sam could see him.

Sam had never seen an angel before. He'd asked Alvin about the paucity of spirits in the world and received a snarky remark about mankind breeding like rabbits. Too many people, not enough spirits to manage them.

The driver ignored Sam's expression, handed him the manifest for signature, then waddled off toward the restroom. His guardian angel didn't follow.

The receiving clerk's shrill voice drew Sam's attention. "Where's this going?" She waved at the pallets.

"Joe Harridan in Marketing." He and Joe had a good-natured feud and this was just the thing to ratchet it up a notch.

"Fine," the clerk said, looking sour. "But you're filling out the Form-5."

Sam grimaced, but nodded. The angel turned and marched through the bay door. Sam followed, trying to look nonchalant. Snow crunched underfoot. Sam folded his arms against winter's chill.

"You have a demon problem," the angel said in a voice that rumbled like thunder.

"Wow, that's direct. What happened to 'Oh my, you can see me?'"

"God works in mysterious ways."

Sam opened his mouth for another sarcastic retort, but the angel's lofty expression made him close it again. He already had a demon problem. Best not to add an angel problem, too.

The angel inclined his head. "I am Tobias. How did you acquire your demon?"

"Nicked myself on an ancient ceremonial dagger when I was still in the Army. I was helping catalog Iraqi artifacts when it happened. My third eye opened, I saw the little twit tormenting a Major, and I freaked out. Drew my weapon and, well, things went downhill from there. Alvin got excited when he realized I could see him, then disappeared. By the time the court-marshal ended, he'd returned claiming he'd been assigned as my personal demon. Like a guardian angel, but in reverse. Any suggestions for getting rid of him?"

"Banish him to Hell with a blessed blade. He shan't return."

"Don't have one of those. Could *you* banish him?"

"My duties lie elsewhere. Were you of the faithful, I would offer a permanent solution involving prayer and supplication. However, I sense little faith within you."

Sam snorted. "Faith is the belief in things unseen. I see this little prat torment me every day. I'm more of a realist."

Tobias gazed skyward, then rumbled a sigh. "I can bless your blade if you have one at hand."

Sam *didn't* have one at hand but pursed his lips as an idea hit him. Making Tobias promise to wait, he dashed inside, snatched an empty folder from the receiving desk, and headed upstairs. He stepped onto the fifth floor at a brisk walk, head down, folder in hand. He'd discovered in the Army that a folder and a brisk pace were a magic shield against idle chit-chat and additional work. Everyone assumed you were doing Something Important and left you alone.

"Sam!" Langowski yelled, spying him from across the room.

Everyone, that is, except the boss. But even he could be fooled by the folder.

Sam waived his manila shield. "Working on it, sir!" Langowski's door slammed shut, and Sam grinned. At his desk, he grabbed his blade—a six-inch medieval sword letter opener he'd bought on a layover in Germany. He used it to add that necessary barbarism when opening official correspondence. One more masterful Hard Working Employee impression and Sam was back in the elevator.

In the loading bay, the driver had his truck's hood up, complaining about a temperamental starter. Sam eyed the angelic claymore thrust into the engine block but refrained from comment and headed outside.

Tobias raised an eyebrow when Sam presented his letter opener. It must have passed muster because the angel laid hands upon it and prayed in Latin. Sam's miniature broadsword glowed brightly before returning to normal.

Tobias placed a weightless hand on Sam's shoulder, sending peace and tranquility through him. "May God bless you on your quest and bring you a little faith." Sam wasn't sure about that last part, but Heaven had just granted him a solution to his demon problem. He wasn't about to quibble.

Sam managed a solemn, "Thank you," before Tobias returned to the truck, withdrew his claymore, and slid into the passenger seat. The driver climbed in beside his unseen passenger and tried the starter once more.

The claymore-free engine roared to life. Sam waved goodbye, and headed inside to slay his demon.

***

Demon slaying in corporate America was more difficult than Sam expected. His tormentor seemed to have disappeared. By the end of the day, Sam's patience had run out. He tucked Faith—which seemed a fitting name for his blessed letter opener—into his suit jacket and went demon hunting. Sam searched three floors before he found Alvin sauntering out of the legal office, whistling a jaunty tune.

That wasn't good.

No matter. It was time to end this. Sam's eyes narrowed, and his pulse raced. The hallway was empty.

He drew Faith and slashed. Alvin screeched and jumped back, clawed hands raised. Faith sliced his palm, releasing something black and gaseous.

"Hey, what's the big idea?" Alvin squawked, then glanced at his palm. "You got a blessed blade?! Oh, shi—"

With a *pop*, Alvin disappeared and Sam was free.

***

Sam rolled into work the next morning whistling Alvin's jaunty tune, his heart light. His whistle trailed off when he found Alvin sitting on his desk, arms crossed, red eyes furious.

"I thought I banished you," Sam said, his throat tight.

"You did." Alvin rose, fists clenched. "HR was ... displeased."

"HR ... on the first floor?"

"*Hell's Resources,* asshole. I'm getting audited because of you."

"But you were *banished.* How'd you get back?"

"Please." Alvin rolled his eyes. "Bureaucracy is my family name. We invented red tape. You think I couldn't short-list myself for a return trip?"

Shit.

Panic blanked Sam's mind. He drew Faith and lunged. Alvin dodged and scrambled over the cubicle wall. Sam had one hand on the wall and a knee on his desk when the elevator dinged, and Langowski stepped out.

"Sam! What the *hell* were you thinking filing a breach of contract against Waters? We just got that account!"

What?

Sam straightened and scowled, remembering Alvin's trip to legal. The little fiend! He sheathed Faith inside his jacket and trailed into Langowski's office. As the door closed behind him, he glanced back.

Alvin was perched atop the cubicle wall, fire in his eyes. He pointed a clawed finger. "I will destroy you."

The door clicked shut.

***

Between the Waters debacle and Alvin's tedious torments, Sam barely survived the week. Langowski threatened to fire him but clearly enjoyed having a verbal punching bag around. Sam kept trying to banish Alvin, but the slippery eel evaded him. By Friday, Sam despaired of catching the little beast. Besides, what was the point? He'd just bounce right back the next day.

Sam was stewing at his desk when a sharp New York accent made him glance up.

"Two pallets of pink paper? Good one, Sam."

Joe Harridan, Sam's rival from Marketing, grinned over the cubicle wall. Joe was tall, muscled, and a favorite among the ladies. Everything Sam wasn't. Sam leaned back and switched mental gears.

"Thought you'd like the challenge."

"I saw you coming a mile away." Joe pinned a pink flyer to the cubicle wall with his fingers. "Langowski just approved our Valentine's Day ad campaign. These babies go out this afternoon."

Sam scanned the pink trifold's beautiful display of Bridewell's office supplies. *Free shipping for the first hundred orders. Call now!* Sam's phone number was printed in large text at the bottom.

"You bastard," he said, admiring the subtlety. He'd have to man his phone all weekend or the campaign would flounder—and Sam would get blamed. It was a slick move, the kind Alvin might think up. Sam glanced around and spied the demon typing away in an unoccupied cubicle across the aisle.

"Takes one to know one," Joe replied cheerily and swaggered away. "I look forward to reading the results in your report. Good luck!"

Oh, yeah. Reports were due. Of all the screwed-up policies Alvin had implemented at Bridewell, the individual weekly reports were particularly insidious—an information overload that supervisors never read, preferring to invent their own lies. It hadn't taken long for Bridewell's employees to turn the reports into a game of creative exaggeration. Sam and Joe were the current battling champions.

Sam eyed Alvin, struck by the demon's intense focus. What was he doing? Sam tip-toed over then froze when he saw the screen. Alvin was typing a report to his superiors in Hell—on a Bridewell computer. Sam frowned. The company network was connected to the Underworld? That explained a lot about the IT department.

Sam slipped back to his desk and opened the share drive. He scanned folders, lips pursed, unsure what he was looking for.

Odd. There was a folder labeled Human Resources and another labeled HR.

*Hell's Resources?*

Sam clicked and received a password request. He leaned back and pondered, fingers drumming the desk. Then he rocked forward, typed "Bureaucracy," and hit enter.

Bingo. Humans aren't the only ones with lazy passwords.

It contained a single folder titled Samuel Davidson Project which held five years of Alvin's reports. Unlike the rest of the share drive, these were neatly organized and—according to the metadata—unopened since Alvin wrote them. His boss never read his reports.

More importantly, Alvin's audit hadn't begun yet. It'd be a shame if those files disappeared.

A maniacal cackle built inside Sam's chest.

Select all. Shift-delete. Why yes, I *do* want to permanently delete all...

No. Not permanently. That was too cruel. Besides, a career of dealing with vindictive bureaucrats had ingrained the importance of keeping copies of *everything*. But he had to do something.

With a quick drag-and-drop, Sam moved the reports to his desktop.

A shriek erupted from across the aisle. "No-no-NO!" Sam spun his chair and watched with wicked glee as Alvin bolted for the elevator. Within seconds, the floor indicator descended to the basement, home of the IT department.

Nice try.

Sam disconnected his computer's network cable with a satisfied sigh. No demonic help desk would find those files now. Freedom was so close.

The office emptied out early, but Sam didn't leave. He'd attracted too much attention to skate out before the boss. He idly read Alvin's reports—such elegant malarkey—until Langowski finally left, taking the stairs.

The elevator slid open and Alvin stepped out, shoulders slumped. The file recovery had clearly failed. The little wretch climbed into his borrowed cubicle's chair and spun around slowly.

A pang of guilt wormed its way into Sam's heart. Perhaps he'd gone too far. But Alvin was a demon. Shouldn't the rules be different?

Sam eyed the clock and shelved the feeling for a moment. He had another problem that needed attention—Joe's pretty pink ad campaign. Sam dialed call-forwarding on his office phone then entered Joe's mobile number. Hopeful customers would start bombarding his rival's phone first thing tomorrow morning. Sam chuckled.

Your move, Joe.

The elevator dinged open, and Sam glanced up. His breath caught at the over-tall demon who ducked through the doors. Sam dropped behind his cubicle wall and peered into the aisle.

The demon was impossibly gaunt, like a stick figure drawn on silly-putty then stretched until his horns brushed the ceiling. He wore a rumpled suit that matched Alvin's and gold-wire spectacles framed his red eyes. Clawed fingers drummed on an oversized clipboard as he scanned the room.

The Auditor had arrived.

The demon lumbered to Alvin's cubicle and spoke with a voice as dry as crumpled ash. "Alvin Bureaucracy?"

Alvin climbed onto the desk and stood eye-to-chest with the lanky demon. "Yes, *Auditor*?" he sneered. Nobody likes auditors.

"Your audit begins now. Should—*when*—you fail, you will be assigned a torment-coach from the Office of Micromanagement for on-the-job training."

Woah. The Office of Micromanagement? And Sam thought human bureaucracy was nasty. Plus, "on-the-job training" didn't sound promising for Sam's demon-free life.

The Auditor droned on. "In the improbable event that you pass, you will receive the promotion you were due"—he consulted his clipboard—"fifty-seven years ago."

Sam stifled a gasp. That was it. Alvin's overdue promotion was his ticket to freedom.

Parchment rustled as the Auditor flipped a page. "Bring up your reports."

Alvin stammered, but Sam popped up like a jack-in-a-box. "Found 'em!" The Auditor spun and blinked at Sam, who gave his most charming smile. "IT must have moved some folders around," he lied and waved at his screen. Alvin eyed Sam dubiously, but stalked over and clambered into his chair. The demon sagged in relief when he saw the reports.

The Auditor gaped at Sam. "You … can see us? Oh, my." He flipped through his clipboard. "There's nothing about that in my files."

Sam smirked. That's what happens when supervisors don't read reports. "Yup, and I'm glad I can. I couldn't ask for a better tormentor than Alvin."

"Really?" both demons said in unison.

"I've learned a lot from this little rascal. He's been making my life a living hell for five years!" No lie there. "Just today I used one of his tricks to ruin my coworker's weekend."

The Auditor's gaze swung toward Alvin, brows furrowed. "Your charge spreads torments on your behalf?"

"That's right." Alvin puffed out his chest, quick to take credit where none was due. "Pitting humans against each other is the epitome of evil."

"Indeed." The Auditor huffed. "This is most irregular." He adjusted his glasses and scanned his checklist. "Hmm. About those reports..."

Sam stepped back as Alvin sailed through his audit, the Auditor bent double to see Sam's screen. He fingered Faith and contemplated banishing them both, but decided against it. Banishment was temporary. This plan would free him forever. It had to.

Finally, the Auditor rose to his full imposing height.

"So, how'd he do?" Sam asked brightly.

"I am ... surprised." The Auditor sighed like crackling embers. "Nobody passes my audits, but Alvin Bureaucracy's files were impeccable." He made a final checkmark and glared at his clipboard as though searching for an error.

Sam wasn't surprised. He'd never met a nastier, more capable bureaucrat than Alvin.

The Auditor tucked his clipboard under an elbow and looked at Sam's tormentor. "I will file the Form-5 with HR for your promotion and reassignment." With another disappointed sigh, the lanky demon lumbered toward the elevator. Eyes bright, Alvin leapt from Sam's chair to follow.

Sam waved. "Good luck on the next assignment!" It had worked. In the name of all that was holy...

The Auditor's clawed hand slapped the closing elevator doors, stopping them. Evil red eyes bored into Sam's. "I have noted you in my report, Samuel Davidson. Expect your replacement tormentor shortly."

Sam's jaw dropped and the door slid shut with a cheerful *ding*.

***

No tormentor arrived over the weekend, so Sam wondered if he'd misheard the Auditor. It was too much to hope for, but hope and Faith were all he had. Driving to work on

Monday, his hand kept drifting toward the blessed blade in his jacket.

He parked in the underground garage and plodded toward the elevators. He'd almost reached them when a gravelly voice behind him asked, "Samuel Davidson?"

Sam jumped and spun. A demon with long tusks and no sense of personal space fiddled with the buttons of his wrinkled suit. "Who's asking?" Sam's hand slipped inside his jacket.

A toothy grin spread across a face that even a mother couldn't love. "Brutus Bureaucracy, your new tormentor. I would have been here Saturday, but HR lost my paperwork. Twice." First-day nerves were obvious in Brutus's rushed speech. "My cousin Alvin assigned me—he's head of Bureaucratic Torments now—and, well, I'm so excited for this opportunity to make your life a living hell."

Sam's jaw clenched. No. Not again. He whipped out Faith and stabbed Brutus Bureaucracy in the shoulder. The demon looked at the blade in surprise before disappearing with a *pop*.

***

Clarissa Bureaucracy arrived the next day, a hulking horned gorilla who caught Sam outside the restroom. He hadn't slept well and overcompensated with coffee, so his bladder was ready to burst. He didn't have time for niceties. Sam banished the cheerful Clarissa before she even finished her introduction.

Desmond Bureaucracy was more cautious when he arrived on Wednesday. He approached Sam's cubicle while a coworker bent his ear about her grandson's adorable puke—complete with pictures. Sam was contemplating the comparative joys of a root canal when his new tormentor caught his eye. Desmond introduced himself over the old woman's prattling before skittering away.

Clever. Sam couldn't stab the demon with a coworker watching. Swinging a sword around the office, even a miniature one, was frowned upon in corporate America. Still, Sam cornered Desmond the next day and banished him as he pilfered a Form-5 on its way to accounting.

The following week Sam banished Eugene, Francisco, and Gloria Bureaucracy. None were around long enough to provide more than annoyance-level torments, but this was getting old.

He arrived early on Friday and found Alvin sitting on his keyboard, arms crossed. His old nemesis looked pissed.

"You have to stop banishing my cousins. The Auditor is crucifying us!"

Sam hoped he was being figurative. "Stop sending them. You're the head of Bureaucratic Torments now. You can end this."

Alvin ran clawed fingers through his comb-over. "I can't. You impressed the Auditor and caught the attention of HR. Everyone wants to torment you!"

Sam fought the urge to banish the little twit and leaned against his cubicle, arms crossed. "So, I'm doomed to eternal torment because I helped you?"

"Well, living torment. The state of your eternal soul is still in question."

That made Sam pause, but he wasn't prepared to debate theology with a demon. He glared. There was only one way out.

It was time to make a deal with the devil.

"I don't have to banish your cousins," Sam said, and Alvin perked up. "Could you assign another cousin to me and then redirect them without Hell's Resources noticing?"

”I *am* the master of misdirected paperwork.“ Alvin's nasal tone was both cocky and cautious.

"Good. I don't care where they go so long as I don't see them. They can drink mimosas in Tahiti for all I care. I'll write their reports, giving every appearance of creatively perpetual torment, while you set up a rotating vacation schedule for your favored cousins."

"Won't work. Demons from outside the family have already elbowed their way into the Department of Bureaucratic Torments. They'll notice."

"Okay. Make the interlopers supervisors. Send them up here to check on your cousins, and I'll banish them back to Hell. That will reinforce your need for resources while removing troublemakers from your ranks." The little devil's eyes sparkled as the idea took hold. "You'll expand your empire, protect the family name, and get credit for tormenting me, while I"—Sam drew Faith and brandished it at Alvin—"will be free from you. Forever."

Alvin blanched at the blessed blade before Sam returned Faith to his pocket and asked, "So, do we have a deal?"

***

The devil is in the details. Alvin should have paid closer attention when Sam sold his time instead of his soul. Sam carefully noted when the little cretin stopped reading his reports, then employed the digital form of his manila shield trick—with an added twist. He maintained his Hard Working Employee ruse, ensuring that files appeared exactly on schedule, but completely changed the tenor of their content.

He told the truth.

The reports became a confession of their deal—complete with a running tally of the demons banished on Alvin's behalf. Sam signed them "Demon Slayer" and each report reached a single, inescapable conclusion.

Tormenting Samuel Davidson was not in Hell's best interests.

Hell's Resources would eventually notice the rising number of banishments and stop sending demons. Then Sam would be free. Until then, he would hunt demons and write his reports. He'd learned how to fight Hell's Bureaucracy—from the inside and with proper documentation—and reveled in the challenge.

Knowledge wasn't a curse. It was power.

<u>*Bonus Story: The Birth of Alvin Bureaucracy*</u>

*As of this writing, I've worked for the U.S. Army for over twenty years as both a soldier and a civilian, and—despite what you may have heard—life as an Army logistician is not glamorous. It's a lot of paperwork and bureaucracy. So, when my (at the time) three-year-old daughter asked what Daddy did at work, I told her the truth: I fought bureaucracy in all its forms. Some days I won, many days I lost, but every day I donned my uniform and fought on.*

*She took me literally. In her three-year-old mind, Daddy fought a slathering monster at work called 'Bawakasy.'*

*One day as I left for work, I knelt to say goodbye. I expected an exuberant toddler hug, but instead she presented her wooden sword with the solemn intensity of the very young. As she passed her sacred blade to my outstretched hands, she gazed deep into my eyes and said, "Slay the beast."*

*I swore that I would.*

*A few weeks later, I needed to run to my office on a Saturday for ... something bureaucratic that really shouldn't have been necessary on a Saturday. As I left, she begged to come along. Who was I to say no?*

*My daughter came dressed for war. Boots, cloak, shield, sword, and a rainbow tutu along with the scariest war face*

*I'd ever seen. Yes, I have a picture of that outfit, complete with war face. You can probably find it on my social media with a little digging.*

*We lived in Germany at the time, and my office was on the third floor of an office building typical of post-WWII German construction: big and blocky with flaking plaster and a steep red-tiled roof. The halls were empty and dark, lit only by dim emergency lights. I keyed into my office, and my daughter stormed past me, sword drawn, and demanded, "Where's Bawakasy?"*

*What could I do? I couldn't tell my daughter—my little knight who believed so fiercely that Daddy engaged in mortal combat every day with the fiend Bureaucracy—that it was all a lie.*

*Though, in reality, it wasn't a lie. Merely a version of the truth. A version she could understand. Anyone who has worked in government service or corporate life can tell you: there are few enemies so insidious as Bureaucracy. Who wouldn't appreciate the opportunity to fight back with a bared blade?*

*Before I even flipped on the light, I dashed behind my desk. The sword on my wall (because of course I have a sword on my office wall; doesn't everybody?) glinted in the* dim emergency light spilling from the doorway. The blade slipped into my hands, pommel cool and heavy. A blessed blade keen to exact vengeance upon my most fearsome foe.

I pointed to the empty hallway, exclaimed in terror, and together we dashed off to fight the slathering monster Bureaucracy.

It was glorious.

Thus was one of my favorite characters born: the demon Alvin Bureaucracy. "Hell's Bureaucracy" was the first short story I ever wrote, and it earned an honorable mention from *Writers of the Future* and was later published in Unidentified Funny Objects 9 (Nov 2022).

Alvin returned in glorious snark in "Death and the Taxman," the first story in Grimsworld Tales. Of course, when I expanded that short story into the full-length novel, I had to add Sam and his family also, who have become fixtures of the Grimsworld trilogy.

Alvin's cousin Brutus has also made guest appearances in "Rare Find! Cordelia's Apothecary Supply" and in Book 2 of Grimsworld: Death and the Dragon (2025).

# RARE FIND!

A BELL JANGLED AS Cora stepped into Harwood's Herbs and Healing. Cinnamon, incense, and a slight undertone of body odor washed over her. She grimaced. Okay, more than an undertone. Fred and Judy Harwood, the shop's middle-aged proprietors, were naturalists who firmly believed in the power of crystals, herbs, and oils over more modern contrivances like deodorant.

But they were the best mediums in Colorado Springs, if you could believe Yelp. Cora had known them for years and was a regular customer but had never participated in one of their séances.

She'd never needed to before now.

Judy was tall and willow-thin behind the counter, her clothing a riot of tie-died confusion. A red rat's nest of dreadlocked chaos flowed down her back and fit perfectly with the shop's general air of cluttered intrigue. Cora wished she could pull off that level of casual flair. The best she'd managed today was a flowered dress that hid her recent weight gain.

A sad smile blossomed when Judy saw Cora, and she slid out from behind the counter, arms spread wide.

"Oh, sweetie. I heard about your daughter. I'm so sorry!" Judy said with her pleasant Irish burr. She wrapped Cora in a crushing hug.

Tears threatened—they were always right there, lurking under the surface since Abigail had died—but Cora pushed them back and disentangled herself. "Thank you. That's why I'm here."

A ghost of confusion flittered over Judy's expression. "Shopping therapy? We have some new charm bracelets from a local artist."

"I think I'm good for now." Cora displayed her wrists with a clatter of jewelry, half of which she'd bought right here. "No, I need to apologize to Abigail. It was my fault she died. My fault she was even driving in that God-awful storm. I need closure. I ... I want you to do a séance for me."

Judy flinched. She glanced around as though looking for eavesdroppers, though Cora was the only customer in Harwood's Herbs and Healing. "We, uh, don't do that anymore."

"But I checked. On Yelp—"

"Old listing, dear. Ever since the Penrose incident..." Judy swallowed and shook her head. "I'd never seen a demon before, and I never want to again. Besides, Fred tossed our arcane supplies years ago. We were never more than dabblers in magic, but we've sworn it off."

Cora plucked a smoky quartz crystal amulet from a shelf. Its tag proudly proclaimed: *Magical Amulet—Wards Against Negativity*. "But half the jewelry you've sold me claims to have magical properties!"

Judy's expression became slightly hunted. "Those aren't *true* magic. Oh, they're effective in their own little ways. Perfectly harmless little things whose value lies in whether or not you *believe* they'll work. I believe, so they are magical for me.

"True magic, however, works regardless of belief. It requires ancient artifacts, incantations, and the intervention of gods, devils, angels, and demons." Judy's Irish burr thickened. "It's the demons that worry me."

Tears came, bringing that empty hollowness to Cora's chest that she'd been fighting for weeks. Her fists clenched, heavy rings grinding against each other. She swiped at her eyes and said, "Please. Abigail was my everything. You have children. If your daughter were torn away from you without warning, wouldn't you move Heaven and Earth for just one more moment? A chance to say goodbye? That's all I'm asking."

Judy bit her lower lip and glanced aside at a picture hanging behind the register. A smiling young couple with a toddler posed before a waterfall. Not just a mother, Judy was a *grandmother*, though she didn't look a day over forty. Cora was fifty-six without any grandchildren yet, despite having three kids in their twenties.

No, two kids. *Damn it!* That familiar emptiness settled into Cora's chest. Death had come too soon for her youngest. It still didn't seem real ... and it was all Cora's fault.

Judy's gaze came back to Cora. Silence fell between them before she shook her head, mumbling something that sounded like a Gaelic expletive. "Fred is going to kill me for saying yes!"

***

Fred wasn't homicidal, but he wasn't happy either.

"No!" He slapped his paperwork-strewn desk for emphasis, jumping up from his chair. The back room of Harwood's Herbs and Healing was a mixture of storage room and office with only narrow aisles between haphazardly piled boxes. Fred was shorter than Judy, just at eye-level to Cora, with loose linen clothes, a bald head, and a scraggly graying beard that reached his chest. He and Judy looked like peas in a pod with the same naturalist flair. And smell.

No, not quite the same smell. Faint traces of marijuana permeated the room. But Fred hadn't partaken recently. His eyes were bright and fiery. He glared at Judy. "Did you tell her about the Penrose incident?"

"Not the details, no, but we'll be more careful this time."

Fred turned to Cora. "We were supposed to summon the spirit of Spencer Penrose, one of the founders of Colorado Springs. He built the Broadmoor resort—"

"I know who Spencer Penrose is," Cora interrupted. "I was raised in the Springs."

"Right. But did you hear the legend about his buried treasure? Yeah, me neither. He spent a couple of fortunes building this town, so I doubt he had anything left over to bury. Anyway, about seven years ago a couple of treasure hunters showed up wanting a séance with Spencer Penrose. To ask about his hidden treasure. We normally dealt with bereaved spouses and old ladies whose dogs had died, but they offered a lot of money." He shrugged. "We took the cash."

Fred leaned forward, fists planted on the desk. "I wouldn't normally admit this, but you need to understand what you're asking for. Those séances with the old ladies? They were scams. Oh, we occasionally felt the presence of something 'other,' but no spirits ever appeared. Mostly we just told the bereaved what they wanted to hear with a bit of showmanship."

Cora's eyes narrowed. "But what about the demon?"

"I'm getting to that." Fred scratched his jaw, which made his scraggly beard stick out to the sides more than it already had. "We decided to give the treasure hunters a real show. Used every artifact we had, not really caring whether they were supposed to be part of the spell." Fred swallowed hard and glanced at his wife. "Nobody was more surprised than us when the séance worked perfectly. Spencer Penrose's spirit appeared right there." He pointed toward a spot on the floor that was buried in boxes. "We'd never seen a full apparition before."

Hope lurched into Cora's chest. "So, you can do it? You can summon Abigail?"

Judy nodded, but Fred squirmed. "We had ten seconds with Penrose," he said, "before a demon rose and dragged his soul screaming back to wherever he'd been. Hell, I suppose." He shuddered but his wife shook her head.

"We were careless," Judy said, "which opened the door for the demon. If we follow the spell to the letter—with the right artifacts—I know we can summon Abigail's soul without demonic intervention."

"No!" Fred yelled again, throwing his hands up.

Judy leaned over the desk. Her voice hardened. "We're doing this, love."

Fred's jaw clenched and his beard fluffed out around his lips. "I still got the spell book, but I ditched the artifacts."

"I'll get your artifacts," Cora said. "Whatever you need."

Judy and Fred looked at her with surprise.

"I have a knack for finding things on the internet. Give me a shopping list, I'll fill it."

Fred grunted. "eBay and Amazon don't carry magical artifacts. Not real ones."

Cora cocked an eyebrow. "You'd be surprised."

Fred's eyes narrowed. He stepped out from behind the desk and edged between boxes to a bookcase at the room's far side. He dug behind a box labeled HOMEMADE WHISKEY in hand-scrawled letters and retrieved a small book bound in aged leather. Parchment crackled when he opened it.

"Ah ha!" Fred said. "First item on the list: Saint Patrick's Cross. Find that on eBay!"

"Okay," Cora said. "That's a fairly common emblem."

"No, not a *replica* of his cross. You need one that Saint Patrick *himself* blessed."

Cora smiled and fished among her many necklaces. "Like this one?" She held out a heavy iron cross deeply engraved with Celtic knots. "Abigail found it at an antique shop in Dublin during her year abroad. She refused to tell me how much it cost, but she wore it every day afterward until..." Cora's throat closed around the words. She swallowed. "And now I wear it." She let the cross drop back onto her chest. "Next item?"

Fred deflated a bit and glanced at his wife. Judy wore an 'I told you so' expression. He sighed. "I'll, uh, make you a list."

***

Half an hour later, Cora sat in her kitchen with her laptop, a cup of black coffee, and an oversized yellow sticky note in hand. Dim sunlight dulled by oppressive clouds shone through the narrow windows bracketing her breakfast nook. The neighbor's dog was out again, barking his head off behind the wooden fence just beyond the window, but Cora ignored him. She eyed the shopping list.

Was she really going to do this? To summon Abigail from her final rest just to say goodbye?

The gaping emptiness in her chest told her that yes, yes she was. Cora needed closure. She needed to apologize. The only reason Abigail had been driving out in that damned storm was because Cora had asked her to stop by Harwood's Herbs and Healing on the way home to pick up a new bracelet she'd ordered. It was a stupid reason to die, but the flash flood had come from nowhere and swept Abigail's car off the road. Taken her without warning.

They'd recovered Abigail's body, but the bracelet was lost. It tore Cora up that she even *thought* about that stupid bracelet.

It was selfish, Abigail deserved whatever peace the afterlife brought, but Cora *needed* to see her. She needed to apologize.

And she needed to do it before she ran out of vacation days.

Tax season had ended and audit season was in full swing. As an IRS auditor, Cora should have been neck-deep in tax returns. The problem was that she couldn't focus. Hadn't been able to think about anything but Abigail for the past three weeks.

Everyone said that time healed all wounds, but they were wrong. Time didn't heal pain like this. It only dulled it. Healing came through acceptance, Cora knew that, but she couldn't accept that Abigail was dead and gone. Not yet.

She sipped her coffee, letting its bitter bite ground her. Warmth suffused her chest as the coffee worked its calming magic. Life always seemed better, more controlled when Cora had coffee in hand. She sighed.

Time to shop.

The first two ingredients on her shopping list were easy. She could pick up heavy candles and incense at Hobby Lobby. The next two were a bit harder.

*Salt from the Irish Sea, one pound,* and *Peat from an Irish Bog, forty pounds.* Clearly, Fred's spell book was Celtic. But did she really need *Irish* ingredients?

Could she risk being wrong just to save a few bucks?

Not with the threat of a demon showing up.

It took two hours to find a vendor in Liverpool, England, who sold local salt from the Irish Sea. Sure, it was from the English side of the sea, but that shouldn't matter. Right?

Irish peat, unfortunately, wasn't so easy. Ireland had banned peat exports years ago. Some vendors still offered Irish peat, but they looked sketchy. Could she trust that it truly came from Ireland?

Cora tapped a fingernail on her coffee cup. Why would a spell for talking with the dead require *forty pounds* of peat? What was so special about Irish dirt? She should have asked.

She continued clicking through websites.

Wait, there was a vendor who looked legit. She scrolled through his page, eyes narrowed. He was an importer who'd gotten a big shipment of peat before Ireland enacted the ban. Perfect.

Crap, he was a wholesaler. He only sold to businesses.

Okay. So, Cora needed a business tax ID. Those were easy enough to acquire.

Step one: set up a Limited Liability Corporation.

Cora snorted and opened a new browser tab. Finally, her years of auditing fraudulent tax returns were going to come in handy. Not that *she* planned to flout the law to import Irish dirt. No, her days of crime were far behind her.

She was just going to skirt the law's edges.

***

Twenty-four hours later, Cordelia's Apothecary Supply LLC was alive and well and doing international imports of Irish dirt and Irish salt. With expedited shipping, everything was expected by Saturday.

She'd picked up white tower candles and spiced apple incense sticks that morning after breakfast. Only one item remained on the list: the cursed ceremonial dagger.

It seemed slightly off that a simple séance would require blood—that's not how they did it in the movies—but Fred and Judy were the experts. If it connected her to Abigail, even for a short time, Cora was willing to trust the magic.

It took all day and several pots of coffee before Cora concluded that a cursed dagger simply wasn't available on the internet.

Fred would have chortled to hear her admit that!

The sun edged toward Pike's Peak outside the windows. Sunset's warm glow filled the kitchen as Cora dug through obscure and sometimes sketchy websites.

The internet was rife with replicas, knockoffs, and cosplay weaponry, but nobody had genuine cursed artifacts. There were lots of old blades, but nobody wanted to advertise that their antiques were cursed.

No surprise there, just disappointment.

Cora's research did, however, land her on an interesting page. *The Lost Treasure of Spencer Penrose.* The treasure hunters who'd paid the Harwoods to summon Penrose's spirit had given up on their quest, but they left the webpage up as an odd bit of history. The page outlined the clues they'd followed, their disastrous séance with Penrose and the demon, and how the trail had gone cold. They claimed that the Broadmoor Resort's management had rebuffed their inquiries, but Cora read between the lines.

They were scared. Other treasures beckoned, treasures without demons attached, and they were happy to leave this one a mystery.

Cora clicked a link labeled ABOUT THE PENROSE TREASURE.

Spencer Penrose built the Broadmoor Hotel in an Old-World style and insisted on installing genuine European fixtures. Most famous of his imports was the Golden Bee, an English pub that had been shipped panel-by-panel over the Atlantic. Reassembled at the Broadmoor, the Golden Bee began a new life in the shadow of the Rocky Mountains. The pub was a favorite haunt for locals and tourists alike and Cora had been there often in her younger days.

Her lips pressed together. It was also where her ex-husband Earnest worked, which was why she hadn't darkened the Bee's doorway in years. He insisted on being called Earnie these days, a vain attempt to recapture his youth as he played the field.

Cora shook away painful memories and sipped her coffee.

The treasure hunters claimed that Penrose had an untold number of missing artifacts hidden somewhere on the grounds. Artifacts now worth millions of dollars. Their source of information was a single shipping slip they'd discovered.

Cora clicked the document image and scanned the list of items. Her breath caught.

There it was, what she'd been looking for: Item #274, Cursed Ceremonial Dagger (Egyptian).

Bingo. The last artifact she needed for the séance was right here in Colorado Springs. She just had to find it.

But how?

There was only one person she could ask for information. The last person she wanted to see.

Jaw clenched, Cora thrust herself up from the table. It was time to go see Earnest.

***

The Golden Bee was crowded for a Wednesday night. The air was light, full of laughter and conversation, and overlain by the decadent smell of fish and chips perfectly prepared. The fixtures were dark oak with the smooth sheen of great age, from the heavy tables and chairs to the paneled walls. A hand-carved oaken bar braced the left side of the room, backed by a mirrored wall that reflected light from antique brass chandeliers. Little banistered shelves lined the mirror, displaying the Golden Bee's more expensive liquors.

Carefully curated bits of Britain decorated the walls: framed newspaper articles, Guinness and Jameson signs, a picture of the Queen (God rest her soul), and a poster that said, "Keep Calm, and Carry On."

Even the low music was some British punk rock band, a playlist chosen to evoke nostalgia for a life none of the patrons had ever lived.

Cora waved her way past the hostess stand and headed for the bar. Earnest—she refused to call him Earnie—was mixing drinks and chatting up a pair of pretty blonde tourists half his age. Despite the age gap, the two girls seemed to hang on his every word.

The years had added gray highlights to Earnest's temples, making his carefully unkempt shoulder-length black hair look dashing. He was untamed yet refined. Even his smile wrinkles looked handsome. It was completely unfair. He wouldn't have looked half that good if *he'd* born and raised three children. The bastard had left soon after Abigail was born, leaving Cora to—

Cora reined in her bitterness and sat next to the tourists. She needed information from her ex-husband, and honey always worked better than vinegar. Especially with Earnest.

He poured two cosmos, raising the shaker with a long and glorious pour. In a fun bit of showmanship—and without glancing at Cora—Earnest's free hand plucked an embroidered bumblebee sticker from a roll and flicked it her way. It stuck to Cora's dress. How did he do that without looking? The embroidered stickers were a Golden Bee tradition, something to make the tourists smile, but Cora didn't feel like smiling. She didn't know what she felt, her stomach a roiling knot of emotions at seeing Earnest again after so many years.

Gaze still focused on finishing his pour, Earnest asked, "What'll you have, love?"

She cocked an eyebrow. Since when did Earnest have a British accent? Pretentious cad.

"You missed Abigail's funeral, asshole."

Oops. So much for starting with honey.

Earnest's gaze snapped to Cora's like a fox caught in the henhouse. He fumbled the shaker. It dropped, shattering the martini glasses in a spray of vodka and cranberry. The tourists shrieked and jumped back as their overpriced drinks splashed onto them. A light mist of smoothly tart cosmo reached Cora, and she grabbed a napkin to wipe her face.

Earnest scrambled to catch everything and shoved it into a sink. He glared at Cora, a look she returned with interest. Grabbing a towel, Earnest dabbed the girls' delicate wrists with profound apologies.

Dark satisfaction filled Cora, followed by annoyance. At herself. That was *not* how she wanted to start this conversation.

"This round's on me, ladies," Earnest said in that fake accent as he wiped up the mess. He started mixing again, and the girl next to Cora glanced over.

"Who was Abigail?"

That familiar ache surged up Cora's throat. She swallowed. "Our daughter."

The girls gave the expected reactions. Raised eyebrows, delicate mouths shaped into little O's, and quick murmurs of, 'I'm so sorry for your loss.' Yeah, everybody was sorry. It didn't help.

The two girls exchanged glances, glared at Earnest, and then at some unspoken signal slid off their stools. The nearest one placed a hand on Cora's arm and leaned close to whisper, "Give him hell."

Now *that* was a sentiment Cora could appreciate.

The girl squeezed Cora's arm in a comforting way and then they were gone.

Earnest glared at her. "Was that really necessary?"

Cora sighed. Honey, not vinegar.

But it was so hard.

"I suppose not," Cora said, meeting his glare. "And I wasn't really surprised that you didn't show up to Abigail's funeral. Just disappointed."

"I had to work."

Work? He'd missed their daughter's funeral to tend bar and *flirt*? Frustration boiled into anger that Cora struggled to push down. She wasn't here to start a fight. She drew a calming breath and glanced at the beer taps behind Earnest. "I'll take a Guinness."

"What?"

"You asked what I wanted. I don't expect you to apologize for being, well, *you,* so I'll take a Guinness."

Earnest brushed his hair behind an ear. He eyed Cora for a second, then turned to the taps. They didn't speak while he poured. Guinness takes time to pour right, and if nothing else, Earnest was a fantastic bartender. Finally, he turned and presented Cora with a pint glass sporting a cheerful-looking toucan and midnight-dark beer.

Cora wrapped her fingers around the cold glass. "Thank you." She drank deeply, then sighed. Deliciously smooth. She pulled the bumblebee sticker off her dress and stuck it onto the pint glass next to the toucan.

Earnest crossed his arms. "So, why *are* you here?"

Cora set down the pint. "Are you still running the Spencer Penrose Society?" It had never been much of a society. Just a few local conspiracy theorists with an unhealthy fascination for the city's founding father.

His eyebrow arched. "Yeah. What about it?"

"You ever hear about a missing Penrose fortune somewhere on the Broadmoor grounds?"

His eyes widened. "Yeah," he said slowly. "There's ru-mors among the staff."

Bingo.

"And where do those rumors say the treasure is hid-den?"

Earnest cocked his head to the side. "Unbelievable."

"What?"

He rolled his eyes. "After all these years, I thought maybe, *just maybe,* you'd come to your senses and stopped by to patch things up. But no, you're on some kind of *treasure hunt!*"

Cora reared back. "Come to my ... *what?* You're the one who left me!"

"You drove me away!"

"You were cheating!"

"You turned cold after Abigail was born."

Red-hot anger burned in Cora's chest. "It's called postpartum depression, asshole. And I needed a partner, not betrayal!" Without thinking, Cora flung her pint at Earnest's head.

He ducked, the bastard.

The pint smashed into the mirror behind him. Leaded glass spiderwebbed and wobbled as though trying to hold itself together before it came crashing down.

That mirror had been made long before safety glass was invented. It had survived the long, hard journey across the Atlantic and over a century of constant use, but it was no match for a pint glass pitched with a wife's righteous anger. Massive shards devastated the alcohol displayed behind the bar. Glass and liquor went everywhere. Earnest leapt back, barely avoiding the worst of it.

The Golden Bee went silent. Well, except for the music. Adele crooned about setting fire to the rain.

All eyes turned toward the bar.

A stepped liquor display shelf sat behind the shattered mirror; an original part of the bar that had been hidden. Though tarnished with age and neglect, the display had the same brass and mirrored opulence of the rest of the Golden Bee.

An antique lacquered jewelry box sat amid glass shards and dust. Its front was painted with the Broodmoor's stylized B.

Cora's breath caught. Yes, she was indeed on a treasure hunt and that looked *very much* like a clue.

Earnest saw it too. He hissed at her not to move then flashed his patented smile toward the crowd. It only took him minutes to empty the Golden Bee. Meals were comped, vouchers were given, and apologies were profuse. As he herded the last customer and the wait staff out the door, Cora ignored his instructions and retrieved the lacquered box. Wet glass crunched underfoot as she set it gently on the bar.

Earnest was an abrupt, looming presence over her shoulder. She glanced back. Instead of the anger she expected, his eyes glowed with excitement. Of course. He was the head of the Spencer Penrose Society. Finding a hidden treasure behind his bar must be like Christmas.

Brass hinges squeaked as Cora lifted the lid. The musty scent of dry-rotted fabric wafted out. A hexagonal mirror flashed on the lid's underside, set in plush red velvet. The box contained only a single item.

A brass hotel room key.

Its jagged teeth resembled the Rocky Mountain ridgeline behind the Broadmoor, rising and falling in a silhouette that Cora would have recognized anywhere. The key's shaft was as long as her forefinger and attached to a brass tag of matching size. The number 221B was stamped on the tag. The B was the same stylized Broadmoor emblem that was on the lacquered box.

Cora reached for the key, but Earnest snatched it first. The tag and key clinked together as he examined their prize.

"221B?" Cora asked, resisting the urge to grab the key.

Earnest smirked. "Penrose was a fan of Sherlock Holmes. Of mysteries in general, really, though I doubt we'll have to go as far as Baker Street in London to find the lock this fits."

Cora jumped when the front door to the Golden Bee slammed open. A thin man with perfect hair and a pin-striped Armani suit stormed in.

"Earnie! Who the *hell* do you think you are? Nothing closes on property without *my* authorization!"

Earnest swore under his breath and spun, palming the key behind his back. "Mr. Bennett! We had an accident, lots of broken glass. I cleared everyone out for safety." He waved his empty hand toward the bar while his other hand slipped the key into his pocket. His phony British accent was gone, but that smooth confidence in his own BS was pure Earnest.

"Accident?" Bennett sneered. "More like an argument with your ex that damaged Broadmoor property!" His gaze swiveled toward Cora. He had piercing blue eyes.

She raised her hands. "I'm so sorry. I was just—"

"I don't care about your squabbles." Bennett cut her off with a wave. "I *do* care about the Broadmoor's reputation, and I hate doing damage control. But guests are upset, so here I am. "His gaze flicked back to Earnest. "You're fired, Earnie. You were on thin ice before, but there's no talking your way out of this one. And don't expect a final paycheck after this mess. Expect a bill."

Earnest's jaw clenched and for a moment he looked like he might take a swing at his boss, but Cora's ex merely drew a deep breath and stepped around Bennett to disappear through the front door.

Cora gave Bennett another quick apology and hurried after Earnest.

***

Outside, the late spring night was cool and breezy, but not unpleasantly so. New leaves rustled overhead and the wind plucked at Cora's dress. Earnest was ahead and to the right, turning onto Lake Avenue. Long strides carried him away from the residential area that surrounded the Broadmoor and toward the resort's main campus on the edge of town, nestled in the shadow of Pike's Peak. Cora jogged to catch up, Abigail's heavy Celtic cross bouncing among her necklaces.

"Where are we going?"

Earnest glared at her but didn't slow. "We? There's no 'we' anymore. You just got me fired!"

"Then give me the key, and I'll leave you alone."

"Oh, no! You're not getting this beauty!" Earnest pulled the key from his pocket and waggled it, making the tag rattle.

"Then I'm not leaving. I need what that key unlocks."

Earnest stopped abruptly on the streetcorner. Across the street, the Broadmoor's expansive lawns and walkways were lined with trees underlit by decorative sidewalk lights. The night was still young and couples strolled along the paths toward dinner or drinks or just to enjoy the pleasant evening. Earnest turned toward Cora, away from the lights, and his face dropped into deep shadow.

"Why?" he asked. "Why do you suddenly care about the lost Penrose treasure? Need more baubles to wear?" He grabbed Cora's wrist and shook it, making her bracelets clatter. She pulled back, breaking his grip, and crossed her arms.

"No. I need a dagger."

Earnest's lips pursed. "Haven't you stabbed me in the back enough times?"

"I … what? No!" Cora growled deep in her chest. "I need it for a séance to talk to Abigail. I—" That heavy lump rose in her throat again. She thought about just grabbing the key and running but stopped herself. Barely. She drew a shuddering breath and said, "I miss her terribly. I … I just need to say goodbye."

Earnest's anger drained away, and his shoulders slumped. "Oh." He ran his fingers through his hair. "A séance? You believe in that crap?"

"I do. Do you remember the Harwoods?"

"Yeah."

"They run an herb shop up in Manitou Springs now. They've done séances before." She snorted. "They even summoned the spirit of Spencer Penrose."

"Really? Huh."

"Yeah. And Judy is confident that they can call up Abigail. *If* I can find the ingredients and artifacts for the spell.

The last item I need is a cursed dagger, which is listed on the manifest of the Penrose treasure.”

Earnest grunted, chewed his lower lip for a moment, then stepped onto the crosswalk. “Okay. Let’s do it.”

Cora had to jog again to catch up. “What happened to ‘there is no we’? And slow down, you long-legged-lummox! Short legs, remember?”

Earnest’s fist clenched around the key, but he slowed. A little. Then he sighed, and his shoulders relaxed. When he spoke, his voice was soft and low. “I’m sorry I missed Abigail’s funeral. I really did have to work. Mr. Bennett doesn’t give two rat hairs about his employees. He threatened to fire me if I missed a shift.” He sighed. “I should have come anyway. Abigail deserved more than an absent father. I just ... thought I’d have more time to patch things up with her.”

Cora’s jaw dropped before she could catch it. That was the first apology she’d heard from Earnest. Ever.

Maybe he was finally maturing in his middle age.

Her jaws clicked shut, and they walked in silence up the long tree-lined sidewalk toward the Broadmoor’s main entrance. The hotel loomed beyond the end of a long oval drive to their left. Cora eyed Earnest sideways.

"So where *are* we going?"

"We're getting a room."

"*What?* We are *not*—" Cora spluttered, but Earnest held up the key again.

"Room 221. Seems a logical place to start looking for whatever this key unlocks, right?"

Cora's jaws clicked shut. Again. How did Earnest always manage to get under her skin so thoroughly?

Honey, not vinegar.

She nodded sharply. "Good idea. But the hotel doesn't use skeleton keys anymore. How do you plan to get into the room?"

Earnest pulled a keycard from his back pocket. "I've got a master key."

"Why would a bartender have—" Cora started and then considered the blonde tourists at the bar. God knows how he got the key, but Cora knew *why.* He grinned, and she shuddered. They mounted the hotel steps. No, Earnest hadn't matured at all. "And if the room's occupied?"

"Remember Linda Rosenberg?"

Cora tripped and caught herself on Earnest's arm. She let go immediately and stepped back, eyes wide. Earnest smiled broadly and pulled open the hotel's etched glass doors with a mocking bow.

Cora did not step inside.

Linda Rosenberg was an alias Cora had used once, decades ago. Back when they'd been young, stupid, and dating. Money had been tight, and Earnest had hatched a scheme to fleece rich tourists staying at this very hotel. It was brazen, exhilarating, and terrifying. And it had been the first and *last* time that Cora intentionally broke the law.

Her ex clearly had no such reservations. He straightened with an inquiring raised eyebrow, the door still held open.

Cora needed that dagger, but could she run a con to get it? What if they got caught?

It didn't matter. Abigail was worth the risk.

Cora's jaw clenched and unclenched. She swore softly and stepped through the door.

***

The hallway outside room 221 was expansive. High ceilings, plush carpets, and expensive art made it feel more like a castle than a hotel. The twining grapevines on the wallpaper looked almost hand painted. Even the air smelled luxurious, fresh and lightly perfumed with lilac. A guest would be hard-pressed not to feel at ease as the hallway ushered them into their extravagant accommodations.

Cora was not at ease. Her heart pounded as Earnest knocked on the door. She was too old to be running a con. They were going to get caught. Sent to prison. God, she was going to get fired! Barred from government service. The IRS wasn't great, but it was a dependable paycheck. What the hell was she doing?

Nobody answered.

Cora drew a shuddering breath and glanced at Earnest. He was calm as a larcenous cucumber, though he was bouncing on his toes a bit. He was loving this.

Cora hated adventure. She'd bought into the whole 'opposites attract' thing when she married Earnest, and they'd made it work for a few years. Long enough to have three kids and to get her *almost* through her accounting degree. But they'd been too fundamentally different. His cheating had merely been the final straw.

A door down the hall opened and Cora jumped. Earnest chuckled, and then finally keyed into room 221.

No one was in, but the room was clearly occupied. Clothes and fishing gear hung on the chairs and desk.

The door swung ponderously closed behind them. The knot in Cora's chest eased.

They were in. No con needed. Just a bit of breaking and entering.

Oh, God. She was absolutely, 100 percent, going to prison.

*Get a hold of yourself, woman! Focus.*

"Right," she said with forced calm. "Let's find a lock to match that key."

The opulent room was well-appointed, as expected from a deluxe five-star hotel. More plush carpets, designer curtains, and a king-sized bed that looked soft enough to swallow Cora whole. White crown molding and chair rails framed peach-toned wallpaper the color of a Colorado sunrise. Yet, despite the opulence, the room wasn't enormous. Those rooms were on the upper floors.

It only took a minute to glance behind all the mirrors, desks, and dressers. Nothing but plain walls. Earnest started tapping walls to see if perhaps their door to 221B had been plastered over.

Cora stood back, glancing around the room. The only piece of furniture they hadn't looked behind was the oak wardrobe. It was massive, carved to match the bed beside it, and bolted firmly to the wall. She swung the heavy double doors open and pushed aside the guests' garments. Three wooden panels greeted her, separated by palm-wide trim boards. She stepped inside to knock on them.

Solid.

Solid.

Echo?

Cora held her breath. She knocked again, comparing sounds before pushing behind an expensive silk dress to run her fingers along the edges of the right-hand panel.

"I got nothing," Earnest said from near the windows. "You?"

"Maybe," Cora said, kneeling to pluck at the trim on the bottom of the panel. It shifted. "Give me the key." She thrust a hand out of the wardrobe. There was silence, then soft footsteps on the plush carpet before the brass key slapped into her hand.

Cora pushed the key's tag under the loose trim and twisted. The wood resisted for a moment then popped free.

Centered under the panel sat a keyhole beside a small brass tag that matched the one in Cora's hand. 221B.

Cora glanced at Earnest, and he grinned at her. Just like in the old days.

Okay, maybe *all* adventure wasn't bad. Her treacherous heart reminded her of the good times they'd had together, and Cora's lips twitched into a matching smile.

Her smile froze at a click from the hallway. The room door swung open. Earnest leapt into the wardrobe beside Cora. He pulled the doors, which swung silently shut on well-oiled hinges. A sliver of light shone into the wardrobe.

"Give me five minutes to change," a young woman's voice said with a sultry purr. "I'll be there before the drinks arrive." There was a pause. "A cosmo. Mwah!"

Cora stared wide-eyed at Earnest. They were trapped! Why the *hell* had she agreed to this?

Earnest gestured furiously—but quietly—toward the keyhole.

Cora inserted the key and tried to turn it. Nothing happened. After more than a century of neglect, the lock was stuck. She wiggled the key back and forth, making scratching sounds that seemed to echo in the tight space.

There was a groan and a pair of thumps from in the room. "God, I hate hiking boots!" Soft footsteps trailed into the bathroom. A wooden toilet seat clunked against porcelain and then...

Cora gagged at sounds she never wanted to hear. Earnest snorted, smothering a laugh. Cora tried not to listen and twisted the key hard in its lock.

The lock shifted, but nothing opened. Back and forth she twisted, working through decades of rust and grime before finally there was a click behind the panel.

Earnest gently pushed on the aged wood.

These hinges were *not* oiled. There was a short but piercing screech, and he froze.

Silence from the room outside. Had the woman heard?

The toilet flushed, and both Cora and Earnest pushed the panel as hard as they could. It screeched open to reveal a narrow landing on twisting stairs. An old servant's staircase.

Earnest pushed past Cora and descended rapidly. She pulled out the key and stepped onto the landing.

The wardrobe doors swung open, revealing a young woman as naked as the day she was born. She looked no older than Abigail was.

Had been. Damn that lump in her throat!

The young woman saw Cora and froze for half a second. Her eyes bulged and she shrieked, leaping back to cover herself.

Unsure what else to do, Cora waved apologetically, said, "Sorry, wrong room," and slammed the panel shut.

***

The narrow stairwell was pitch black and smelled of mildew and dust. Spiderwebs clung to Cora's fingertips as she felt her way down into the darkness. From Earnest's quiet but heartfelt cursing, she realized that he was blazing a trail through the worst of the webs.

The thought of angry spiders seeking retribution on her ex for their destroyed homes made Cora smile in the darkness.

The smile dropped when something tickled the back of her neck. With a shriek and a shudder, Cora swiped at her neck and stumbled downward.

She slammed into Earnest's back. He grunted, and Cora fell back onto the stairs. There was a flash of light ahead of her.

Earnest waved his cellphone around, revealing drooping spiderwebs over bare lathes. He turned the light on Cora, blinding her for a second, before descending once again.

Cora kicked herself for being an idiot. She slipped her phone out of her pocket—all dresses should have pockets in her opinion—and thumbed on the flashlight.

The air cooled as they descended, raising goosebumps on Cora's arms. They passed three more landings before reaching a door at the bottom. It was larger and heavier than the servant doors into the rooms, and its hinges shrieked like a dying soul when Earnest shouldered it open. By Cora's calculations, they were at least two stories underground.

Cora gasped as they shone their lights around the room. It appeared to be an old kitchen turned warehouse. Wooden crates of all shapes and sizes filled the large room. Industrial stoves and sinks from the 1800s lined the wall to the left while marble-topped counters lined the back and the right. A heavy door in the center of the back wall matched the one they'd entered.

The largest crates were stacked in the center of the room, with smaller crates on the counters. Dry rot and pests had taken their toll over the decades, littering the floor with dust, debris, and rat droppings.

"It's real," Earnest murmured, eying the crates. He chuckled. "I'm gonna be rich!"

"Good luck claiming it," Cora said, stepping forward to examine the nearest crates.

"Whaddya mean?"

"You think the Broadmoor will grant you claim to treasure found on their property? To an employee they just fired?" She ran fingertips along the rough wooden crates. They were stamped with inventory numbers and shipping data from around the world. England, India, China.

"Well, I'll smuggle it out!"

Cora arched an eyebrow and waved her light toward a flat upright crate taller than she was. "I almost want to see you try." She pointed at the inventory numbers. "We're looking for item number 274. The dagger may be in an Egyptian crate."

Earnest huffed and scowled but shone his light over the crates. He went right and Cora went left.

They found numbers 270-293 stamped on a small crate in the back of the kitchen. The box was rough wood, dry rotted and barely holding together. The lid fragmented under Cora's fingers as she tore it off, splintering around the nails that had held it together.

Inside were packages wrapped in heavy brown paper and packed in cotton. The crate smelled of mildew. Cora reached for the first package and gently unwrapped it.

It was a small and heavily tarnished silver chalice.

She set it aside and reached for the next. A statuette of Bastet, the Egyptian cat goddess.

The third package was awkwardly heavy at one end. Cora unwrapped it. Her breath caught and Earnest whistled.

They'd found it.

The cursed ceremonial dagger was over a foot long with a narrow wicked-looking blade. The cross-guard was gold overlain with sapphire that sparkled in the cellphone light. Four cobras twined up the hilt in silver and gold, their hooded heads forming the pommel.

"This is it," Cora said, throat tight. "The last artifact we need to talk to Abigail." She glanced at Earnest and tears came unbidden. For once, he had no snide remark. He swallowed and nodded.

Voices and footsteps sounded from the stairwell. Cora's head jerked up. She glanced back. Light shone in the doorway, growing brighter.

"Shit!" Earnest spun, looking around desperately.

Cora rewrapped the dagger and clutched it to her chest. "We have to run."

"I'm not leaving my treasure!"

"It's not yours!" Cora moved toward the back door. "I have what I came for, and *I'm* not staying around to get arrested."

Earnest cursed again, grabbed the statuette of Bastet, and joined Cora at the back door. Six heavy iron bolts held it secure.

Cora wrenched the first one back with a scream of tortured metal. She pulled the second. The third.

"Broadmoor security!" a man's voice yelled from the stairs. "Stop where you are!"

Cora did not stop. Neither did Earnest. Together they unbolted the door and pulled it open.

A wall of lathe and plaster greeted them. They were trapped.

Cautious footsteps approached. "Don't move." Cora glanced back, heart pounding. Four men in suits blinded her with powerful flashlights. She squinted but didn't see any weapons.

"No," Cora said and threw herself at the plaster wall.

***

Escaping the Broadmoor was more a matter of stealth and cunning than speed. At least for Cora it was.

They broke through into a parking garage. Her ex, once again looking out for number one, sprinted up the ramp without looking back. Cora grimaced, shaking plaster from her hair. She wasn't surprised, but his quick abandonment hurt all the same. She couldn't hope to keep up. Instead, she ducked behind a nearby BMW that probably cost five times what her Peugeot did.

She crouched, pulse pounding in her ears as the security guards pushed through the hole she'd made in the wall. She held her breath, afraid they'd glance over at her, but the guards sprinted after Earnest without looking her way.

Footsteps faded up the ramp. Cora drew several calming breaths, then tried the BMW's door. It was unlocked. This was valet parking. The key was in a cup holder. She grinned.

Why run away when you can drive?

Cora glanced in the rearview mirror and grimaced. She looked like a wreck, plaster-dusted with her hair sticking out at odd angles. Every instinct screamed at her to escape, but Cora slid back out of the car to brush herself off. She fixed her hair in the BMW's side mirror then flashed herself a smile. It looked more frantic than confident.

It would have to do.

Cora pulled out of the parking garage, forcing herself to drive slowly, as though she hadn't a care in the world. She drove once around the property before easing up to the Valet Parking stand by the Broadmoor's main entrance. Her nerves jangled, urging her feet to *run,* but she stamped down the impulse. Breaking and entering and looting lost treasure were enough crimes for today. No need to add grand theft auto to the list.

A courteous young man took the key from her and drove away.

Cora drew another calming breath, squared her shoulders, and walked as sedately as possible toward the Golden Bee's parking lot. No scrambling security guards chased her down. No police sirens sounded in the distance.

Had Earnest gotten away? The paper wrapping around the heavy dagger crinkled in Cora's grip as she walked with measured steps.

This séance with the Harwoods had better work.

***

On Saturday morning, Cora was back at Harwood's Herbs and Healing with a heavy cardboard box of séance supplies. It was early yet, but black clouds made the day darker than it should have been. The weather had turned yesterday, heavy with the scent of rain and foreboding. It was the kind of day designed for curling up on the couch with a cup of coffee and a book.

Well, Cora's coffee was in a travel mug in the box. The book would have to wait. Today was about saying good-bye.

Today was about Abigail.

None of the shops on Manitou Springs' main street were open yet, but Judy came at Cora's knock. She let Cora in and together they wove through the store to the back room.

Cora's eyebrows rose. The room had completely changed. Gone were the boxes and supplies. The furniture was pressed against the walls. Fred knelt barefoot on the floor, chalking in the final touches to a six-foot-wide summoning circle. The white chalk was stark against the aged hardwood. The circle contained a six-pointed star formed of two triangles with each intersection bound by an intricately drawn Celtic knot.

Fred glanced over his shoulder and rose as Cora entered. His tie-dyed shirt and linen pants felt somehow wrong for a séance—and for the weather—but Cora refrained from comment. They were the experts. Fred carefully stepped out of the circle.

"You found everything?"

"I told you I would." Cora set the box on the floor, then knuckled her back as Fred rummaged through it. He straightened, pulling out the forty-pound bag of Irish peat that had been at the bottom.

"Oh, yeah! I've been trying to find this stuff for years! How'd you get it?"

Cora smiled. "You can find anything on the internet if you look hard enough. What's so important about Irish dirt? Do we mix it with the salt to spread around the circle?"

"Nope." Fred lugged the bag of peat to his desk against the wall, stepping around the circle. "This'll be perfect for the whiskey I'm making!"

"*What*?" Cora said. "I imported Irish dirt so you can make ... *whiskey*? That crap was expensive! I had to create an LLC just to import it! What about the séance?" Her fists clenched, and her bracelets rattled. "What about Abigail?"

Judy laid a calming hand on Cora's shoulder. "You'll talk to Abigail, don't worry. But we don't work for free, especially considering what happened last time with that demon."

Fred nodded emphatically. He sniffed at his expensive Irish dirt, sighed happily, and returned to the box of supplies to set everything out. Candles, incense, Irish salt—also ridiculously expensive—and Abigail's Celtic cross necklace. The dagger he left in the box.

Cora fingered the necklaces that remained on her chest, feeling the absence of Abigail's cross.

A heavy knock hammered on the shop's front door.

"Ah!" Judy said, stepping back into the shop. "I wondered if he'd show."

"He?" Cora grabbed her travel mug from the box and followed Judy.

Earnest stood outside the glass door.

"Oh," she said. "Him."

The rain had started, just a drizzle but picking up. Earnest didn't seem to notice. His hands were shoved into his jeans pockets, and he looked like he hadn't slept in the three days since Cora had seen him. Judy unlocked the door and waved him in.

"So," Cora said, grip tight on her coffee. "You escaped the Broadmoor."

"Not really." Earnest ran fingers through his lanky black hair. Damp from the rain, it curled at his neck. Damn, he looked good. The aged punk rocker bad boy. No wonder the tourists at the bar hung all over him. Cora scowled as pleasant memories of those fingers running through her hair rose unbidden.

"Broadmoor security caught me halfway across the lawn," Earnest said. "Dragged me into a back room where Mr. Bennett gave a convincing mobster act." His voice rose into a nasal falsetto that sounded nothing like his former boss. "'You stole from us Earnie. From the Broadmoor. Do you know what we do to thieves?'"

Thieves? Cora's heart fluttered. Had Earnest the bad boy given her up? Were the cops coming? Oh, God.

Cora took a fortifying swig of coffee. It was hot, black, and bitter. Perfect. "So, what did Bennett do?" Look at that, her voice didn't even crack.

Earnest snorted, shoving his hands back into his pockets. "Nothing. Oh, he was full of bluster and threats, but once Bennett figured out what we'd found in that old kitchen, that we'd discovered the lost Penrose treasure, his tone changed *real* quick. He offered me a deal."

Cora arched an eyebrow. Earnest's shoulders sagged.

"No criminal charges in exchange for a binding non-disclosure about the Penrose treasure. They even took that little Egyptian cat statue. I got nothing."

Cora eyed him. He hadn't mentioned her to Bennett. Had he? She had to know. "Did you...? Am I..."

A ghost of a genuine smile appeared. "Did I rat you out? Come on. You know me better than that. But I'd avoid the Broadmoor for a while. They pulled a crappy picture of you from surveillance."

Cora sighed in relief. Then her eyes narrowed. "That was three days ago. You could have at least called to let me know you weren't in jail."

Earnest grunted as though the idea had never occurred to him. It probably hadn't.

Cora shook her head. Earnest had his moments, but he was still an inconsiderate ass. "So, why are you here?"

Judy answered that one. She'd leaned against the cash register while they talked, gaze flicking between them like a spectator at a tennis match. "Earnest called yesterday. Asked when we were doing the séance."

He nodded, gaze locked on Cora. "You're not the only one who wants to say goodbye to Abigail. And for everything I went through so you could get that cursed dagger, it's the least you owe me."

Cora's jaw clenched, hackles rising at the suggestion that she owed him *anything*, but she didn't argue. He hadn't ratted her out and for once, Earnest was right. Despite his faults, he still deserved the chance to say goodbye. Abigail was his daughter too.

Fred called from the back room. "Ready when you are!"

Cora extended a hand to Earnest. "Come on. Let's go say goodbye to our daughter."

***

Cora stood beside Earnest as Fred and Judy walked around the salt-lined circle, waving incense sticks and chanting something that was supposed to be Celtic, but sounded Latin. Flickering candlelight underlit everything. Six oversized candles sat upon the chalked Celtic knots. Abigail's cross—the cross blessed by Saint Patrick himself—sat in the center of the circle, a beacon to summon her spirit from the afterlife.

The incense that Fred waved smelled more like marijuana than the spiced apple Cora had picked up at Hobby Lobby.

Fred stopped between Cora and Earnest and presented the cursed dagger, narrow blade held upright. Cora pricked her finger on its sharp point. She hissed. It hurt more than she'd expected. A drop of red blood rolled down the blade. Earnest did the same, their blood mixing as it slid downward. The snakeheads on the cursed blade's pommel looked alive in the flickering candlelight, eager for more blood.

Fred and Judy stopped chanting, and Fred flicked the blade toward the circle. Drops of mixed blood arced downward and landed beside Abigail's cross.

A white wall of light shot up around the circle's edge. Cora jumped back, hand to her chest. This was it.

The rotten-egg smell of brimstone was Cora's first clue that the séance had gone horribly wrong.

"Um, Fred?" she said, but he didn't hear her.

"Abigail Knowles," Fred intoned, "by the blood of your parents, I bid you come forth!"

The hexagonal center of the six-pointed star flashed white. A hideous figure rose into view as though riding an elevator. Small horns curled atop a head more wrinkled than a prune. Oversized tusks jutted from the creature's lower jaw, and he wore a gray suit that was wrinkled enough to look appropriate in an IRS office, especially around tax time.

Fred froze, wide-eyed. Judy screamed. Earnest stumbled back from the circle.

Cora had never seen a demon before. Her hindbrain wanted her to run screaming in terror.

The demon sighed a long, low, rumbling sigh. Tired red eyes flicked around the room before settling on Fred. Or, more accurately, on the dagger in Fred's hands.

"What?" the demon said in a gravelly voice filled with long-suffering. "What do you want?"

Fred's lips flapped like a fish. He dropped the dagger, which stuck point first into the wood floor, and backed away.

Cora reigned in her gibbering terror and glared. "Who are you and where's my daughter?"

"I am Brutus." The demon glanced around the circle, red eyes taking in the salt, the candles, and Abigail's cross between his feet. Brutus twitched when he noticed that and carefully stepped away from it. "Usually, humans call the police when someone goes missing. Not Hell."

Cora's chest tightened, and she found it suddenly very hard to breathe.

Hell. Abigail was in Hell?

No, she couldn't be.

Cora shook herself. She waved at the circle. "Abigail died. Thus, the séance."

Brutus snorted and mimicked her gesture. "Séance? This is a Celtic summoning circle if ever I saw one. Someone mixed up their spells."

Cora *knew* a séance shouldn't require blood! She glared at Fred and Judy, who had huddled together in the far corner.

Earnest plucked the dagger out of the floor. He leaned toward the circle's glowing white wall and brandished it at the demon. "Bring us Abigail's spirit!"

Brutus snorted. "Or what? You'll stab me? *I* cursed that dagger millennia ago for a priest of Ra. Threatening me with it is like threatening me with my own left sock."

He didn't have socks, or shoes, and his clawed toes scraped at the hardwood. Earnest turned the dagger in his hands and for once seemed at a loss for words.

A heavy, hollow emptiness filled Cora, stealing her breath. It was sorrow too deep for words, too deep for tears. After everything she'd done to reach this moment, she'd failed. Abigail wasn't coming. She was gone and Cora would never be able to say goodbye, to apologize for getting her daughter killed.

Cora's jaw clenched. No. This wasn't the end. It couldn't be.

She glanced at Fred and Judy. They didn't seem inclined to help.

"If we can't compel you," she said to Brutus, her breath only hitching a little, "then perhaps we can make a deal. What do you want?"

Earnest hissed, "Are you *crazy*? You can't make a deal with the devil!"

Aw, look at that. He really did care. She leaned in and hissed right back. "I will give anything for a chance to see Abigail one last time. To say goodbye and"—her breath caught—"to apologize for getting her killed." Earnest jerked back at that. She hadn't told him that she was the reason Abigail had been out in the storm.

Brutus cocked an eyebrow at her, shoving the wrinkles in his forehead to one side. "Are you offering your soul?"

Okay, perhaps not *anything*. "No."

"Good. We have a surplus at the moment. It's probably a paperwork glitch, but Torments has been overrun with damned souls lately. We had to expand the Customer Annoyance Department just to make room."

Customer Annoyance? Cora decided not to ask.

Brutus's nose suddenly twitched. His posture straightened, and he paced around the circle, sniffing. His gaze flicked across the marijuana-infused incense Fred had dropped before settling on the desk against the wall. The desk where Cora's coffee cup sat.

A look of longing filled those red eyes.

Cora knew that look. She felt the same way every morning before her first cup. Could her deal with the devil be *that* simple?

"Bring us Abigail," Cora said, "and I'll give you the coffee."

Brutus twitched and blushed as though caught committing some carnal sin. "I, uh..." His jaws snapped shut. He shook his head, though his eyes remained focused on the coffee cup.

Damn. Of course it wouldn't be that easy.

"Bring us Abigail's spirit, and I'll make you a fresh cup of coffee every morning for the next year."

Brutus's eyes bulged. He practically salivated, but again shook his head.

"Two years."

"I..." He gulped. His voice lowered to a whisper. "We aren't allowed coffee in Hell."

Cora retrieved the travel mug. She popped its lid next to the summoning circle's glowing wall. Delicately, she blew the steam toward Brutus. He inhaled deeply with an expression of beatific bliss.

"Okay," he rumbled. "You have a deal. Hold on."

Brutus dropped back through the floor, disappearing as though he'd stepped off the edge of a cliff.

***

As soon as Brutus disappeared, Fred and Judy scrambled out of their corner. "I told you this was a bad idea!" Fred screeched. "Destroy the circle before it comes back!"

"No!" Cora stepped between them and the still-glowing circle. "Abigail is coming. Don't you *dare* take this away from me. From us. "She glanced back at Earnest who had squatted on the floor, staring blankly at the cursed dagger in his hands.

Judy shook her head. "It's a demon, darling. In our shop. Our home! We never should have agreed to this."

Cora eyed them both. Determination stared back at her.

Fred leapt forward, trying to get past Cora. She shoved him—*hard*—and Fred fell on his ass away from the circle. Judy yelled and dodged past Cora's other side. She spun back to shove the taller woman, but she still had her coffee cup in that hand. Judy twisted past.

There was a blinding flash of white light followed by darkness.

No, not darkness. Not quite. By the feeble, flickering glow of candlelight Cora saw Judy's foot. It had slid through the Irish salt, breaking the circle.

Cora screamed. "No! NO!" She grabbed Judy and yanked her away from the circle, but it was too late. The damage was done. Cora stared without really seeing, fists clenched. She wanted to scream, to howl, to punch someone really *really* hard!

Abigail was gone. She'd been close, on her way. And then she was torn away. Again.

Grief overwhelmed Cora. She dropped to her knees and tears poured out. Judy's arms wrapped around her. Cora tried to push away from Judy—this was *her* fault!—but her strength drained away. Cora curled in on herself, sobs wracking her body.

Abigail was gone.

"Mom?"

The tremulous voice cut through Cora like a knife. She spun out of Judy's arms. There, in the center of the dead summoning circle, stood Abigail. Brutus loomed behind her, looking nervous. Abigail was dim, a literal ghost of her former self, but she was here. Undercut hair streaked with blue was pushed over her left ear. She had Cora's dark brown eyes and Earnest's easy smile. As though the entire world was a joke that only she understood.

A choked cry tore from Cora.

Her daughter was here.

"Abigail!" Cora scrambled forward on hands and knees.

She stopped short when Brutus stepped forward. He raised a clawed hand and pointed at the circle's broken edge.

"You would cheat Hell?" he growled, gravelly voice angry.

What? Cora followed his accusing finger to her travel mug. It lay on the floor. A chill traipsed down Cora's spine. She didn't remember dropping it. The nearby salt was stained brown from spilled coffee.

"I'm sorry. It was an accident."

Brutus didn't look amused. And he was no longer contained by a summoning circle. He growled. "You promised me coffee. A deal was struck!"

"Three years!" Cora gasped. "I'll make you a fresh cup of coffee every day for three years! No, a pot. A whole pot just for you. Just, please, let me talk to Abigail. Please."

Brutus's smile shifted his wrinkles to bare sharp teeth. Cora supposed it was a smile because he chuckled. "I take it black and strong enough to strip paint off a pitchfork."

Cora forced herself to match Brutus's smile. "Me too. I'll summon you tomorrow at seven o'clock sharp."

Brutus nodded and stepped back.

And then there was nothing between Cora and her daughter's spirit. Nothing but silence and regret.

"I..." she said. Words wanted to tumble out, but they got all mixed up. Cora's carefully rehearsed speech wisped away like incense. "I'm sorry," was all she managed.

A sardonic half-smile lit Abigail's eyes. "Me too. Being dead sucks."

"No," Cora said, struggling to her feet with a clatter of jewelry. "I mean, it's my fault you died. You never should have been driving in that storm. I—"

"Bullshit, Mom."

That pulled Cora up short. Earnest stepped up beside her. "Don't talk to your mother like that!"

Abigail rolled her eyes. "Hi, Dad. Glad to see you too. It's been ... how many years?" She glanced between them. Her forehead scrunched. "You two aren't, I mean, you know..." Abigail trailed off, looking embarrassed and unsure of whether she wanted an answer.

Cora's eyes widened. "With him? No! Wouldn't dream of it."

"Good." Abigail crossed her arms while Earnest squawked indignantly. "No offense Dad, I *am* glad to see you, but Mom always had horrible taste in men. You were just the first."

Cora added some squawks to the ones coming from Earnest. "Horrible taste in men?"

"Please. Remember the guy who laughed like a braying donkey?"

"Francis was really quite sweet—"

"And that cop? What was his name? Adonis? He at least had looks, but that guy was dumber than a bag of well-sculpted rocks."

"Really." Cora crossed her arms and glared at her daughter's ghost.

"Anyway," Abigail said. "I guess old prune-face here"—she hooked a thumb over her shoulder at Brutus—"didn't bring me back to analyze your love life." She stepped forward and placed an insubstantial hand on Cora's arm. It should have felt cold, or tingly, or something, but Abigail's touch was merely ... absent. She wasn't really there.

Cora swallowed the lump in her throat. "I'm sorry. It's my fault—"

"No. It. Isn't. I had a nice chat with the Grim Reaper when I died. Call it fate, call it chaos, or call it bullshit, but my time had come. Nobody escapes this world alive."

Cora shook her head. Abigail's endless reserves of pragmatism hadn't been inherited from her parents. "Death came for you too soon," she murmured.

Abigail shrugged. "No argument here, but you'll have to take that up with old rattle-bones himself when you see him."

Cora folded her arms. "I will."

"But Mom, seriously, stop beating yourself up over me. I lived my life the way I wanted to and now I'm ready for ... whatever's next."

Cora wished so desperately that she could give Abigail a hug at that moment. Her arms ached to reach out. She drew a deep shuddering breath.

Brutus placed a hand on Abigail's shoulder, drawing her back. "I must return you before you are missed," he said.

Abigail snorted over her shoulder. "Missed? Nobody even knows I'm there!"

Cora and Earnest exchanged glances. He asked hesitantly, "Um, where exactly are you?"

Abigail shrugged again. "Purgatory? Limbo? Somewhere ... in between, I think. It's got both angels and demons, a ton of dead people, and a whole crap-load of creatures you wouldn't believe! When Brutus grabbed me, I was chatting with—"

Brutus cut her off. "It's time to go."

Abigail nodded. "Right." She glanced between her parents, smile turning sad. "Bye, Mom. Bye, Dad. I miss you both, but—and don't take this the wrong way—I hope I don't see you again for a very long time."

Cora covered her mouth but didn't bother wiping her tears. "So long, Sweetie. I love you, and I miss you more than you know." Earnest didn't say anything. He just nodded numbly, swallowed, and toyed absently with the dagger still in his hand.

Brutus's red-eyed gaze met Cora's. "Tomorrow at seven o'clock. Sharp." He gripped Abigail's shoulder, and they descended through the floor more slowly than Brutus had disappeared earlier. Abigail gave a final wave before she disappeared.

And then she was gone. Forever.

***

A month later, at seven o'clock sharp on a Saturday morning, Cora sipped coffee at her kitchen table while Brutus rose behind her summoning circle's white barrier. The circle was smaller than the one Fred had used, though made with the same materials. Fred and Judy had sworn off magic entirely—again—so Cora had taken everything. Inside the circle sat a simple wooden stool holding a full pot of coffee.

Black and strong enough to peel paint off a pitchfork.

Brutus raised the pot to his nose, inhaled deeply, then rumbled a happy sigh. He settled onto the stool, flipped the pot's lid up with a clawed thumb, and took a deep draught. That much coffee straight off the burner would have scorched Cora's throat, but Brutus merely smiled in satisfaction. He smacked his lips.

"So, where were we?" he rumbled.

Cora took a much smaller sip of her coffee. "You were explaining why I have to summon you every day instead of just showing up on your own." Not that she *wanted* an unrestrained demon in her kitchen, but information was always good to have.

"Right!" he took another deep draught, half-draining the pot. Brutus didn't stay long each morning, but he was surprisingly chatty. Cora got the impression that he led a lonely existence at the bottom of Hell's food chain. "I got banished from the mortal realm by a blessed blade a few years back. Received a century in Torments as an IT customer service rep as punishment." He shivered. "I hate giving service with a smile." Brutus took another fortifying gulp of coffee. "I'd be in it deep if my boss caught me coming to the mortal realm without a proper summons. Doesn't matter that he's my cousin. Alvin's a stickler for the Rules."

"Fascinating. So how are blessed blades different from blessed artifacts?" Cora's gaze flicked to Abigail's Celtic cross beneath Brutus's stool.

Brutus snorted and took another drink. "Well, let me tell you!"

And he did.

After the fiasco of the Harwoods' séance, Cora had decided to learn everything she could about how magic *really* worked. She didn't want to be a practitioner herself, but she loved the idea of helping folks with information and artifacts. She would become a purveyor of the rare and magical, but she needed to understand the how and the why of magic first.

The very idea of real magic was exhilarating. And it *worked.* Seeing Abigail again was proof of that.

Thinking about her daughter still left an aching hole in Cora's chest, but at least it didn't break her soul. Not anymore. Abigail had forgiven her. Or rather, she'd absolved Cora of guilt, and now she was headed for ... whatever the afterlife held. Abigail would be okay. Her daughter was infinitely capable of handling herself.

Earnest, however, hadn't taken the séance/demon summoning nearly as well. He had once again disappeared from Cora's life.

She sighed and sipped her coffee, silently wishing Earnest well. Hopefully, he'd find peace with it all someday.

It was time for Cora to carry on. She was back at work auditing for the IRS and neck-deep in tax returns. But she spent every spare moment away from work researching and purchasing magical artifacts online. Some of them were rare finds, one-of-a-kind items. She had a decent stock now and had finished building her business website yesterday.

Cora smiled as Brutus rumbled on about blessed blades, filing the information away. Once he was gone—and that pot was almost empty—Cora had plans for the weekend. Not a date, especially not after Abigail's painfully honest assessment of her love life, but something vastly more important.

Something exciting and unique. A hobby that was quickly becoming her passion.

Today she would launch Cordelia's Apothecary Supply.

*I genuinely didn't realize how much of a fan favorite Cora was going to become. When I first met her on the pages of "Death and the Taxman," Cora was a charming and sweet side character, nothing more. Then* Writers of the Future Volume 39 *received its first review by the writer, musician, and book reviewer known only as bookmarkedone. She had many nice things to say, but most poignant to me was when she stopped everything to say, "Hankins, if you're listening, I need more Cora!"*

*I was floored. I'd never had someone beg me to write a story before. And she wasn't the only one who loved Cora. Readers came out of the woodwork to gush about this tax auditor and charming mother of three who had turned to the dark arts. Cora had won their hearts.*

*"RareFind! Cordelia's Apothecary Supply" was first published as a stretch goal for my* Death and the Taxman *Kickstarter in 2023. Since then, it has become one of my most-read short stories, second only to "Death and the Taxman." The readers have spoken, and yes, I'm listening.*

*There will be more Cora.*

# VALHALLA AND COCKTAILS

A ghost's afterlife wasn't nearly so good as Garrick had hoped. It was better! Sure, people had a nasty habit of walking right through him, but Garrick was finally taking that tropical vacation to Okinawa he'd always dreamed of. The one he and Lilly had saved for, back before she got sick. Before they both got too old to travel, and Death came knocking.

Garrick shook his head. No need to turn maudlin.

That thought brought a small, sad smile to his lips. Lilly had liked using big words like that. He missed her something fierce but refused to dwell on the painful memories of his lost love. He was on vacation and determined to enjoy himself.

Garrick closed his eyes, stretched out on a poolside lounger, and basked in the South Pacific's glorious sunshine. He let the sounds of splashing water, whispering palm trees, and happy children wash over him.

Okinawa really was heaven, the sunshine literally warming Garrick's soul. Well, maybe not Heaven. As an Odinite, perhaps he should compare it to Valhalla. Whatever. The sunshine on his pasty white legs felt good.

Since becoming a ghost six months ago, he'd managed to touch the physical world only once. He could still feel Lilly's cold tombstone under his fingertips. That cold sadness always returned when he thought of her.

But this place? With its warm breezes, singing birds, and sunsets over the water that looked like paintings? Absolute paradise! Even Valhalla couldn't have compared to Okinawa, though a bit of free-flowing mead would have been nice.

Garrick cracked an eyelid and glanced at the drink beside his lounger. Something fruity in a coconut and shaded by a tiny pink umbrella. What had that guy called it? A Bahama Mama? Garrick had never had one of those before. Hell, he'd never stayed at a Hilton before, but vacation was about trying new things. If he could touch it. Garrick stretched his ephemeral fingers toward the coconut like he'd reached for Lilly's hand back in high school. Full of hope, but nervous as hell.

His fingers passed right through the coconut. He felt nothing but cold from the blended Bahama Mama. No rough coconut shell. No weight in his hand. Nothing. Garrick sighed and dropped his hand back to his lap. Paradise was nice, but he'd give just about anything to touch the world again.

Garrick closed his eyes again, placed both hands behind his head, and resumed basking. It was a good thing ghosts floated. Otherwise, 'laying' on a sun lounger he couldn't touch would have been a might bit problematic. Not that nobody could see him, but the pretense of reality was nice. At moments like this, with his eyes closed and the sun warming his soul, Garrick could almost imagine that he was here in body as well as spirit.

A sudden shadow blocked the sun. Water dripped through Garrick like chilly spears. He cracked an eyelid. A businessman's oversized and Speedo-clad backside loomed overhead, descending like Godzilla on Tokyo.

"Gak!" Garrick yelped. He dropped through the sun lounger like the ghost he was and scrambled back.

The man crashed down with a hearty sigh, the lounger creaking under his weight. He reached for his Bahama Mama, sucked deeply on the straw, and smiled broadly. "Ah, this is the life!"

Garrick scowled. Okay, so it hadn't been *his* chair he'd been lounging in. Or his drink. It wasn't like a ghost could belly up to the bar and order another round. How would he even pay for it?

A crowing laugh pulled Garrick's attention to the small grassy area beside the pool. His eyes narrowed. Mothers lounged on blankets, reading books, or scrolling their phones while ignoring their kids in the pool. They didn't see him.

The long-tailed rooster strutting amongst them did. He was a russet with cream and black highlights streaking his wings. One of them Japanese breeds Garrick didn't recognize, but a beautiful bird with long legs and an arching neck. And he was slightly translucent.

A ghost rooster? Garrick had never heard of a fowl ghost. Visions of being haunted by his farm's chickens sent a shudder through Garrick. The rooster chortled again; its comb flopped over one eye like one of them sloppy hair-dos teenagers liked these days.

"What you laughin' at?" Garrick asked, not really expecting an answer.

The rooster flipped his comb to the other side with a twitch of his head and fixed Garrick with an orange eye. "You're not a very good ghost, are you?" it said in a cultured, pretentious tone.

Garrick eyebrows climbed his forehead. "Yer a talkin' chicken?"

"And you're a lousy ghost," the rooster said. "Your point? And stop gaping. It's rude."

Garrick's jaws napped shut. He stomped toward the chicken. "Wha'd'ya mean, I'm a lousy ghost? It ain't like ghosting comes with a user manual."

"Would you even read the manual? You don't exude an air of literacy." The rooster eyed Garrick up and down. He glanced at himself. His outfit had changed from swim trunks back to his overalls and plaid shirt. His clothes kept doing that when he wasn't paying attention, reverting back to his trusty farm clothes.

Garrick stopped in front of the rude little bird. Well, perhaps not so little. Up close, the rooster was easily twice the size of the ones he'd raised. "I always wondered what chickens on my farm back in Colorado thought about. Turns out, yer just rude for no reason. The nerve, callin' me illiterate. I'll have you know I graduated with honors from Pike's Peak College!"

"My deepest apologies," the rooster said, not sounding apologetic at all. "You are truly a scholar without peer."

Garrick glared at the rooster, trying to decide if he'd been insulted again. He should have just walked away, but this was the first conversation he'd had since he'd died. It wasn't off to a great start. "I'm doin' just fine as a ghost!" he yelled. "I defeated the demon tryin' to drag me to Hell. Chopped his arm off with his own scimitar!"

"Oh, is that what you left over there?" The rooster glanced back toward the businessman. Garrick's sword rested in the shadows under the sun lounger, a spiritual item unseen by the resort's guests. "Rather careless, leaving a cursed blade just lying around."

Garrick glared at the bird. So, he'd left the sword behind. Big deal. He was on vacation! He just kept the infernal thing around in case that blasted demon came back. Regardless, Garrick whirled, stomped back down the line of sun loungers, retrieved his scimitar, and stomped back. It was hard to stomp properly as a ghost, but Garrick gave it his best. He leaned the blade against a palm tree and—annoyingly—it rested against the rough bark just fine, not passing through like Garrick would have. He turned back to the rooster. "You sure talk a big game. Who're you to be lookin' down yer beak at me?"

The rooster cocked his head. "I am Basan." He said it with significance. Like someone might say, 'I am Iron Man.' Maybe it was a cultural thing. Maybe this whole conversation was just a cultural misunderstanding. Garrick reined in his temper.

"Nice to meetcha," he said, trying to sound like he meant it, then added with matching intensity. "I am Garrick Thorsson."

Basan cocked his head again as though Garrick were being particularly dense. "I am ... Basan. The fire-breathing chicken. Spirit Guardian of Japan..." He trailed off and sighed an offended sigh, a sound Garrick had never heard from a chicken before. "Americans. You've never heard of me, have you?"

"Uh, no. Sorry." Garrick shrugged and slid his hands into the pockets of his overalls. "You really breathe fire?"

Basan didn't answer, but fire lit the tip of his tail. Orange and blue flames danced up his spine like he'd flicked on a propane grill made of feathers.

Garrick felt his jaw flapping. He tried to come up with something witty in response, but he never got the chance.

A scream ripped through the air. More screams followed, coming from the touristy shopping area inland from the Hilton. Every head snapped toward the commotion.

Something halfway between a roar and a yell overrode the panicked screams. It warbled with a tone that chilled Garrick's soul. That was a battle cry. Garrick's nerve endings twitched in response and every instinct yelled for him to run. So, he did.

Garrick dashed through the privacy wall toward the screams. He'd always been one to run toward trouble instead of away. He may have been raised a farmer, but he was a warrior at heart, nursed on his mother's stories of Odin and Thor, Freya and Loki. He dashed across the road and slid into one of the shopping center's winding, cobbled alleyways. A panicked throng of tourists and shopkeepers ran right through him.

Unfortunately, Garrick wasn't a warrior in practice. He was working his way upstream through the crowd when he remembered his scimitar. It was still leaning against the palm tree.

He stopped in the middle of the narrow street. Should he go back?

Another battle cry cut the air. The flood of tourists petered off, the last an elderly gentleman who worked his cane as he hobbled away. The empty cobblestone was littered with dropped shopping bags and tumbled clothing racks. In the middle of the street, two shops down, stood a demon with flared batwings. A very shapely demon.

She was tall and voluptuous—another big word that brought Lilly to mind. Garrick shook his head. Not now! The demon wore a form-fitting gray suit that looked kinda like a kimono but cinched with a belt. She had spiky black hair that formed points like hedgehog quills. Fury burned in her red eyes and twin daggers danced in her hands.

A short Japanese policeman squared off against her, only a billy club for a weapon. His partner was already down behind him, a young woman who clutched her stomach with bloodstained hands. The male officer yammered at the demon—Garrick didn't speak Japanese to know what he said—one hand extended in a placating manner that the demon ignored. The poor fella looked ready to piss himself.

Garrick couldn't blame him.

The demon flickered and disappeared, reappearing only ten feet away behind a fallen scarf rack. She screamed again, anger laced with frustration. It was like she'd tried to teleport away like they did in them sci-fi movies but got her coordinates wrong.

The demon's rage boiled over, and she lunged at the nearest target, the poor quivering policeman. She slashed and stabbed with both daggers in a whirlwind the policeman was hard-pressed to defend against. He stumbled backward and tripped over his partner. The man fell. The demon loomed over him, blades poised for a killing blow.

"Hey!" Garrick yelled. "Pick on somebody yer own size!" It wasn't original so far as opening lines went, and Garrick wasn't quite her size, but it did its job. The demon paused. She glanced at Garrick and those furious red eyes narrowed.

"That's right, you ugly sack of spare parts! I'm talkin' to *you*! "Garrick imagined that she might actually be pretty if her face weren't marred by undiluted rage. He jabbed a finger at the demon then paused, his brain finally catching up with his mouth. What was he doing? He couldn't fight this thing! Why the hell had he left that stupid scimitar behind?

The demon charged with a roar, this one more feral than her earlier battle cries. She was only two steps away when Garrick lunged aside and threw himself through the window of a t-shirt shop. One advantage to being a ghost: no broken glass. He hid behind a rack of shirts that said "Party Like a Pirate" as the demon scrambled to a stop. She turned and stepped through the window, shifting from corporeal to spirit with ease.

What Garrick wouldn't give to know *that* trick!

She stalked through the shop, her breath slowing from enraged beast to stalking hunter. The shop wasn't big, but Garrick wasn't confined to the aisles. He slid through and behind racks and shelves, tracking the demon by her breathing.

Now what? He'd saved the two cops, and help was already arriving. Wailing sirens preceded a cluster of emergency personnel running past the window. Heavily armed officers led the way, followed by medics. None of them saw Garrick or the demon inside the silent shop.

Silent. Ah, crap!

A blade touched Garrick's throat, cold and sharp and very solid against his ephemeral skin. He froze, then glanced to the right. His gaze traced up the demon's arm to her red eyes. They were still angry, but the rage was controlled. Calculating.

"Uh…" Garrick gulped, then regretted it when his Adam's apple bumped the blade. He was already dead, so he didn't know what would happen if that blade cut him, but he didn't want to find out. "Sorry about the insult. You, uh, are actually quite pretty. In a modern sort of way. Spiky hair's not my thing, my Lilly's hair was near to her waist when we met, but, you know, you do you and it looks good on you and that's okay. Uh," Garrick realized he was babbling, "heavens to Betsy please don't kill me." He snapped his jaws shut.

The demon's eyes narrowed, her expression turning inward. The blade dropped from Garrick's throat, and she muttered, "What the hell am I even doing here?"

In a blur, she was gone. Like the Flash used to do on TV.

Garrick sagged, drawing deep breaths. After the demon failed to return for a full minute, he slid back through the window onto the street. Emergency personnel were doing their thing with the injured officer, unaware and unconcerned with Garrick's ghostly presence.

The sound of steel on stone pulled Garrick's attention to the right, the direction he'd come from the Hilton. Also unseen by everyone else, Basan was sauntering up the narrow street dragging Garrick's scimitar. When the rooster saw him, he flapped over and dropped the blade with a *clang* at Garrick's feet. Roosters can't roll their eyes, but the tilt of Basan's did the trick.

"Rushing into battle without your sword?" Basan said. "Not only are you a lousy ghost, you're not a very good warrior, are you?"

"I didn't see you rushing in to help," Garrick snapped. He wasn't in the mood for more insults. Problem was, he couldn't disagree with the rooster's assessment. That stung.

But Garrick was a son of Thor, an Odinite sworn to battle for the glory of Valhalla. He scooped up the sword and eyed Basan. "You called yerself a Guardian Spirit of Japan, right?" The rooster nodded with a regal air. "Then stop being saucy and help me protect it! That spiky-haired demon thinks she can run away and cause more chaos? Hurt more people? Not today!"

Garrick stomped past a surprised-looking Basan, headed toward the hotel. "Come on," he said. "I ain't lettin' some bloody-minded fiend ruin my vacation paradise. We're goin' demon huntin'."

***

After two hours of storming fruitlessly through Chatan in search of the demon, Garrick and Basan were walking along the sea wall that led back to the Hilton. The sun was setting, shattering the sky with pinks, oranges, and blues. It was yet another glorious, warm evening with just a hint of a breeze. Seagulls swooped after bugs, and the occasional dragonfly buzzed through Garrick. It was hard to believe that just a couple hours ago there had been a demon attack not three blocks away. The cafes and bars to their right were full of noisy tourists. Pop music mingled with laughter and the crashing waves that rumbled against the rocks to their left.

Garrick glanced at Basan as they walked. The rooster had been uncharacteristically quiet during their trek through Chatan, offering little more than directions when Garrick got lost in the winding streets.

"I'm thinkin'," Garrick said, one hand in his pocket, the other carrying his scimitar, "that we may need a different plan to find this demon."

"Yes," Basan said. "Wandering randomly hasn't done much, has it?"

Garrick's lips pursed, but he nodded. "Thanks fer joinin' me on the hunt. Yer the first soul who's ever seen me..." He paused. "Well, no, there was that one guy when I died. It all happened so fast. A demon wrenched my soul from my corpse and then dragged me through The Grand Estates retirement home chasin' down this other guy whose soul he wanted. Frank Totmann the demon called him. Almost got him too. If it weren't fer Frank's quick thinkin' and my quick hands, I woulda been neck deep in brimstone by now."

Basan cocked his head, fixing Garrick with an orange eye. "Fascinating." Garrick couldn't tell from the rooster's deadpan tone whether he was serious or mocking, but then Basan continued, "What did you do?"

Garrick grinned. "Frank told me to steal the demon's sword, and I lopped the bugger's arm off. The big fella didn't have a lot of fight left after that." He chuckled.

Basan nodded to himself as they strolled beside the ocean. A raucous laugh from one of the bars caught Garrick's attention. Tourists with beer and cocktails were swapping tales of their day's adventures. He missed that. Not the bar—he hadn't spent a lot of time in bars while he was alive, too expensive—but Garrick missed the camaraderie. He'd outlived all his friends. Outlived Lilly. And now he'd outlived himself and was stuck as a ghost wandering the world...

There he went again, bein' maudlin.

Basan pulled Garrick back to the present. "Your story ... explains some things. Despite Japanese views on the spirits of their ancestors, ghosts aren't as common as humans might imagine. Old Grim is rather good at his job of reaping souls and sending them onward."

Garrick snorted. "Yeah, well he forgot to show up fer me."

"And that's my point. When a ghost remains, it's usually because they have some pressing business. Death's scythe sends souls where they're supposed to be, whether that's Purgatory or one of the other realms depending on the alignment of their soul."

Garrick cocked an eyebrow, "Hold up. You believe in Purgatory? I'll admit I don't know much about Japanese religion, but that's a Christian thing, ain't it?"

Basan cocked his head, his comb flipping to the other side. "Religion has nothing to do with. Purgatory serves many realms. A holding place before Judgment."

"Huh."

"That's how death *normally* works. But ghosts are created when their need to remain in the mortal realm exceeds their need for Judgment. Instead of traveling to Purgatory after Grim reaps them, they remain to haunt the living."

"Like moanin' and rattlin' furniture and stuff?"

"In their attempt to communicate, yes. But you," Basan said, returning to his point, "weren't properly reaped. You are an aberration."

Garrick's lips pursed. That was a big word he didn't recognize, but he caught the context.

"So," Garrick ran fingers through his thin hair, "how do I rattle the furniture? I've tried, but for the life of me, I can't touch anythin'!"

"I ... don't know." The words sounded sour on Basan's tongue. "For spirits like me, changing form or turning corporeal is simply a matter of willpower. Like this." Basan's beak snapped forward, and he caught a dragonfly. The thing buzzed briefly, but with a crunch and a gulp, Basan ate it.

Garrick eyed the rooster. Willpower. Well, it was worth a shot. He reached out to touch the sea wall that kept tourists from falling into the ocean. He focused, thinking about how desperately he wanted to feel the rough, damp stone. He willed himself to become solid once again.

His fingers passed right through the surface. He felt nothing more than the sun's warmth on the stone and the cool underneath. Garrick sighed. "Willpower ain't enough for me. So, what's the ticket? How do I touch the world?"

Basan's head waggled from side to side, a motion that implied the chicken equivalent of a shrug. "If you were a normal ghost, I'd ask what was holding you to the mortal realm. There's a connection between their pressing need to fix something and 'rattling the furniture' as you called it, but I don't know what the connection is."

It was Garrick's turn to shrug. "Lilly was my life, but she died before I did. Outside of her, I got nothin'. No terrible secrets or villainous plans. No crimes that need solvin' or pressing needs to keep me here."

Basan didn't reply and they walked in silence, serenaded by the sorrowful cries of the gulls, and illuminated by the dying light of paradise as the sun slipped below the horizon.

***

Basan left Garrick at the Hilton, saying he'd return in the morning, so Garrick wandered back to the market. The crowds had returned with nightfall. The tourist shops were closed, but the bars and restaurants were doing robust business. The area where the demon had appeared was still taped off, but all the cops were gone. Blood stained the cobblestones where the woman had lain. Garrick hoped she was okay. The occasional tourist peered past the tape, but nobody seemed inclined to wander in.

Except for one woman. She was Japanese, short with long black hair held back by a simple leather band around her forehead. Her hair was longer than Lilly's had been. She wore a white silk kimono patterned with a tangled vine of purple flowers and was squatting down to examine the ground where the demon had stood.

Garrick slid through the caution tape and walked toward her. She glanced up. Her dark eyes fixed on his, and Garrick froze.

"You ... can see me?" he said.

She rose, a curious tilt to her head, but her expression remained smooth. "You were here before," she said. Her voice was soft, sultry even, with a heavy Japanese accent. "You challenged Kurai."

"Kurai?"

"The demon."

Garrick stepped forward, drawn by those beautiful eyes. "You know her? How can I find her?" His grip on the scimitar tightened.

The woman stepped closer and suddenly Garrick found himself practically looming over her. He hadn't meant to get so close. She smelled of jasmine tea and cherry blossoms, a light perfume that hit Garrick's senses like a sledgehammer. He tried to step back, but her hand caressed his jaw.

That touch was like lightning. The first woman's caress he'd felt in years. The nurses at The Grand Estates hadn't counted. Their ministrations were purely clinical, necessary for end-of-life care. The last person who'd touched him like that was Lilly.

Lilly.

Garrick jerked back and slammed into a wall. It took a moment for that to sink in. His free hand slapped backward. The wall was solid behind him, gritty with flecking paint. He was touching it, pressing against it, just as the woman had touched him.

How?

The woman closed the gap, her hand again reaching up to caress his jaw. "I must get back," she said softly. Her face was so close that her breath warmed Garrick's cheek. He gulped, trying to focus.

"Uh, back where?"

"To Hell." Her eyes flashed red, full of fury. "And you're going to take me."

Cold steel slid between Garrick's ribs.

***

Darkness swirled around Garrick. The pain of that piercing blade drew him ever downward in a rainbowed spiral that reminded him of the opening credits of Doctor Who, but darker. He'd spent his last couple of years in The Grand Estates unable to do more than watch TV all day. One thing he'd learned was that things never turned out well for people who fell through space-time with demons clinging to them. The vortex spun around Garrick, stealing his breath, his voice, his very soul.

Kurai clung to him like a lover, her limbs wrapped so tight around him that he couldn't have pried her free if he tried. Her dagger remained buried in his side, pressed between their bodies. She still wore the beautiful woman's face, but Garrick knew she was the demon. It was in the eyes.

Space and time snapped back into reality. Kurai released Garrick, dropping to her knees on close-shorn grass, and Garrick stumbled back. His hand flew to his side. The dagger was gone. The wound was gone, though the pain of it still lingered. His gaze snapped back to Kurai.

"What the *hell* was that? You stabbed me!"

She wasn't looking at him. Her gaze flicked from side to side, panic overwhelming her rage. "No. No!" she yelled, surging to her feet. "Not here!"

"Garrick Thorsson!" A booming man's voice spun Garrick around. "Welcome to Valhalla!"

A Viking strode toward them across the grass, grazing goats scattering from his path. Twin axes rode his hips and a horn of mead sloshed in his hand. The smile behind his red beard was broad and welcoming. Behind him loomed a Longhouse that was several stories taller than it should have been and much, much longer. Yggdrasil, the tree of life, overshadowed the Longhouse and was itself overshadowed by stark mountains that circled the valley. The very air exuded a sense of peace and victory, a final resting place for the warriors of legend.

Valhalla.

"Woohoo!" Garrick cheered. "I made it!" He capered around, his worries about Kurai gone, and waved his scimitar in the air. Then he stopped and looked up at the massive Viking who'd greeted him. The man was close enough now that the smell of sweat and mead wafted freely over Garrick.

"Is Lilly here?" Garrick asked. "She weren't much of a warrior, but she fought like hell at the end, and, well, I can't imagine the afterlife without her..." Garrick trailed off at the Viking's expression. It was dark and murderous and aimed at Kurai.

"What's she doing here?"

Garrick turned. Kurai had regained her composure and stood demurely on the grass, hands clasped inside the sleeves of her kimono. If she hadn't just stabbed Garrick, her expression might have looked innocent. He glanced back up at the warrior.

"Well, she's a demon who stabbed me with one of them daggers she's probably hiding up her sleeves. Then she rode me like a bucking bronco all the way here. Not too sure about the *how* of it, but she said I was gonna take her to Hell. "He glanced around at Valhalla's glorious surrounds. "I think maybe she took a wrong turn at Albuquerque."

The Viking shook his head, his gaze never leaving Kurai. "That's not a demon, though her blades are cursed by Lucifer himself. She's a Kitsune. A rage-filled shapeshifter and trickster on par with Loki for devious cruelty. Were you not an Odinite, the cut of her cursed blade would have sent your untethered soul to Purgatory and Hell's front doorstep." He thrust his mead horn into Garrick's free hand and unlimbered both his axes.

Kurai glared at Garrick and muttered a dark curse under her breath. Then she raised a hand toward the Viking. "I have no quarrel with you, Ragnar Lothbrok."

"Then you shouldn't have come to Valhalla!" he yelled. "I will send you back to where you belong!" With a roaring battle cry, Ragnar clanged his axes overhead and then charged Kurai.

She lunged forward to meet him, and as she did, she changed. It was like watching her step through a vertical pool. The change started at the tip of her nose and flowed backward, turning her from a demure woman to a giant black wolf as tall as a horse.

Kurai and Ragnar met in a clash of teeth and blades. Ragnar's attacks were powerful, but no match for Kurai's speed. He chopped and swung. She dodged and bit. A powerful paw crashed into Ragnar's temple, sending him cartwheeling into the open field. He tumbled to the grass, rolled, and shot to his feet with a roar.

A matching battle cry sounded behind Garrick, but louder and from more voices. He spun. An army of Vikings streamed out of the Longhouse, men and women bearing swords and axes and shields and flagons of mead. More voices joined the chorus, screaming their challenge at Kurai the wolf. She crouched, eying the army while keeping Ragnar in view.

The Vikings charged.

Garrick abruptly realized that he stood between the newcomers and their enemy, holding a flagon of mead like a tourist watching a boxing match. He threw back a long draught—by Odin that tasted good!—tossed the horn over his shoulder, and raised his scimitar to join the charge.

That's when Kurai cheated. She changed shape again, this time shifting into a mirror image of Garrick, complete with overalls, scimitar, and dribbles of mead on her chin. She tackled Garrick, taking him to the ground. They rolled in a tangle of limbs before regaining their feet.

The two Garrick's circled each other. It was like looking in a mirror. Every move he made, she mimicked perfectly. The charging Vikings rumbled to a stop in a circle around them. Their faces filled with confusion.

"Which one's the Kitsune?"

"Who spiked my mead? I'm seeing double!"

"Who do we attack?"

From the corner of his eye, Garrick saw Ragnar pop his neck from side to side. "Fell them both. Valhallan blades will send the Kitsune back where she belongs."

Garrick's gaze flicked to the Viking. "Whoa, wait a minute. What about the real Garrick?"

Ragnar shrugged, a rippling motion of muscles and doom. "The real Garrick, whichever you are, will suffer the consequences of bringing a Kitsune to Valhalla."

"But that wasn't my fault!" Kurai shouted in Garrick's voice.

Ragnar said, "Garrick Thorsson shall become a thrall in Valhalla's kitchens for..." Ragnar glanced around as though seeking advice, "...a thousand years?"

The Vikings cheered.

Garrick and Kurai both cursed.

The Vikings charged.

Kurai spun to defend herself, scimitar held low in a two-handed grip. That was her mistake. Garrick lunged toward her, but he didn't stab her in the back. Instead, he wrapped his arms around hers in a bear hug, scimitar still clutched tight in his fist, pinning her elbows to her sides. He was not about to be trapped in Valhalla as a thrall.

Kurai was his only way out.

She twisted in his grip, driving her elbows into his ribs. Garrick grunted but didn't let go. Then the Vikings were upon them, and one threw an axe at Kurai.

It whirled and then struck them both, cutting deep through Garrick's arm before slamming into Kurai's chest. She screamed. Garrick screamed. The axe's momentum threw them backward, but they never hit the grass.

Darkness swirled. The vortex swallowed them again. Though Garrick felt himself pulled to stay in Valhalla, he closed his eyes and tightened his grip, riding Kurai back to the mortal realm like a bucking bronco.

***

They snapped back to reality in the same narrow street in Chatan where Kurai had first appeared, behind a rack of scarves outside a tourist shop. Though Garrick could swear they'd only been in Valhalla for a few minutes, sunrise was painting orange lines atop the tall buildings. The police tape was gone, and the shop owners were reassembling their street displays.

An old woman puttering with the scarves lurched back with a scream when they appeared, her gaze fixed on the wounded Kurai. She couldn't see Garrick. Kurai dropped to one knee, reached back to grab Garrick, and flung him off her.

He spiraled through the old woman and into the shop across the street, coming to rest amidst shot glasses and keychains. He floated there for a moment, regaining his bearings, and checked the cut on his forearm. The Valhallan axe had bitten deep but without blood. Garrick still couldn't touch the world, but he thought about what Basan had said about spirits changing their appearances through willpower. He thought about his arm *not* having a huge gash in it. The cut healed as if it had never been. Garrick grinned and turned back to the window.

The shopkeeper in front of Kurai had stopped screaming. She approached the demon—who still looked like Garrick's doppelganger—and timidly reached toward the axe in her chest. Kurai backhanded the woman, flinging her into the wall.

Aw, hell no!

Garrick stormed through the window, scimitar in hand. Before he reached Kurai, she wrenched the axe from her chest and roared her familiar battle cry. She screamed to the heavens and then her form changed once again. Yet, unlike the last time, this change didn't look controlled and intentional.

Fur, feathers, horns, and scales exploded from within her. It was like all the shapes she'd assumed as a Kitsune were vying for real estate. She became a chimera. A wolf's head with ram's horns and a snake's tongue sat atop an Amazon's body strapped with leather armor. Black bat wings snapped out behind her. Her right arm that clutched the Valhallan axe looked human; the left was all scales and claws. A fox's bushy tail swayed behind her. Only her legs looked normal, hidden by gray slacks over what Lilly would have called sensible shoes, but without the suit jacket. Kurai's twin daggers graced her hips.

Garrick slid to a stop, mouth gaping at the monster before him. Kurai roared again and the few remaining shopkeepers bolted. She stomped toward Garrick, axe pulled back to fell him like a lodgepole pine.

Garrick didn't give her a chance. "Git out of here, you varmint!" he yelled and charged. Kurai blocked his first attack with the axe. He kept swinging, yelling with every blow. "Get. Out. Of. My. Vacation. Paradise!" What he lacked in skill, he made up for in enthusiasm. His last attack knocked the axe from Kurai's grasp.

She caught Garrick's wrist on a backswing with her clawed left hand. "You don't have the power to banish me, worm!" she yelled, then punched him in the temple. Hard.

Garrick's world turned sideways. He dropped his scimitar and sagged in Kurai's grasp, shaking his head against the spinning colors. She grabbed his overalls and wrenched him forward until his nose touched her wolf's snout.

"You're going to wish you'd never crossed me, Odinite," she spat. Her snake's tongue flicked as she talked, tickling Garrick's cheek.

"Ain't my fault you got a bee in your bonnet. Lemme go!" Garrick clutched at her clawed fist. He wasn't breaking that grip. But he'd been in this situation before. He knew what to do.

Garrick released Kurai's wrist and snatched her daggers from her waist. He thrust them upward at the arm holding him and—

The daggers disappeared.

Garrick's empty fists thumped under Kurai's scaled forearm. His eyes widened. His gaze flicked to Kurai's waist. The daggers were right back where they'd been. She smiled a cruel smile.

"You really are a terrible ghost," she said. "No control of the world around you."

"I know, right?" Basan's cultured voice said from behind Garrick. "Whatever shall I do with him?" Surprise flickered over Kurai's face, and Garrick twisted in her grip to look back down the empty alley.

Basan sauntered toward them, claws making deliberate clicks on the cobblestones. His long tail swished rhythmically. The rooster ran his gaze over Kurai. "It's been a long time, Kurayami Kitsune. But not long enough. You are still banished from these lands."

Kurai's snarl deepened. "The Lord of Darkness will—"

"Do nothing!" Basan interrupted, flame flashing in a blue nimbus around him. "Word of your coup in Hell has spread even here. You may have found power in the underworld, but this is *my* realm. I give you but one warning. Leave. Now."

"Yeah, go to Hell!" Garrick yelled. He had to admit, it felt kind of good to say that.

"I can't!" Kurai roared right back. She *shifted* and the world flickered like it had when they'd gone to Valhalla. But instead of traveling to another realm, they just moved a few feet over and reappeared behind the scarf rack. Impotent rage burned in Kurai's eyes. Something was keeping her here. Despite the Kitsune's power, she'd lost her ability to transit realms at will.

Basan clucked at her. "Then run." He opened his beak wide, and flames burst forth.

Kurai's red eyes bulged. She flung Garrick down and disappeared in a streak of light.

Garrick covered his head against the rooster fire that raged briefly above him. The heat seared his soul. Then it disappeared, and he glanced up. Basan cocked his head sharply, throwing his comb over one eye. "Take up arms, Viking. The chase is on!" Then the Guardian of Japan followed Kurai in a streak of flame and feathers.

Garrick blinked at the departing rooster's afterimage then scrambled to snatch up his scimitar and the dropped axe. "For Valhalla!" he yelled, weapons raised. In a streak of denim and steel, he followed Basan the fire-breathing chicken.

***

Garrick wasn't sure quite *how* he knew where Basan was, but he followed the rooster across the island like a magnet after iron. Perhaps the Guardian of Japan was leading him, helping him chase Kurai down to banish her once again from Okinawa. They streaked through towns and farms, along the rocky coastline, and into the center of another city.

Kurai stopped on a broad sidewalk outside a glass-fronted corporate headquarters. Bridewell Incorporated, a name Garrick recognized. One of those multi-national companies that dabbled in everything from paper supplies to guided missiles. The workday was just starting, so a steady stream of employees flowed through the rotating glass doors. None of them saw Kurai. Garrick recognized the slightly translucent quality of a spirit hidden from human view. She had resumed her demon's guise with the formfitting suit, spiky black hair, and flaring bat wings.

Garrick stopped on the sidewalk a dozen yards away. Next to him, Basan was still rimmed in a flaming blue nimbus. The rooster flared his wings and stepped deliberately between Kurai and the flow of foot traffic into the building.

"Keep running, Kitsune. You're not welcome here."

She pulled her gaze from the building and drew her daggers. "I do what I want," she said and went corporeal. She roared her battle cry to the heavens.

And the screaming began, once again. Those nearest to Kurai scrambled away while people on the periphery pulled out cell phones to video the event. Traffic on the busy road screeched to a halt. Drivers either stared goggle-eyed or abandoned their vehicles and ran.

Basan turned corporeal as well and crowed. The crowd gasped as his call echoed in the urban canyon. More cell phone cameras appeared. He flapped his wings and blew a stream of flame toward Kurai. Her wings snapped closed in front of her like a shield. The rooster's flames curled around her, heating her wings from black to deep orange, but she didn't burn.

Garrick turned his face from the heat of Basan's fire, stepping back. The flames roared, then died. Garrick heard a meaty *thunk*. Basan flew back, tumbling in a ball of flaming feathers. He rolled to a stop against Bridewell's windows, and his flames sputtered out. One of Kurai's daggers protruded from his chest.

"You're no Guardian," she said, gaze fixed on the rooster. "You're nothing but a chicken ready for the barbecue."

Then she strode through the glass, phasing through it like the spirit she was, though she remained visible to the world. The watching crowd inside scattered in her wake.

Garrick knelt beside Basan. The rooster fixed him with a pain-filled eye. "Stop her," he said, voice laced with pain. "Banish the Kitsune before she hurts more of my people."

Garrick's grip tightened on his weapons. "I'll try."

Basan coughed. "Don't try. Do."

"Aw, come on! Now yer just quotin' Star Wars!"

Chicken faces aren't designed for smiling, but Garrick could have sworn he saw a wry grin. "Lucas was quoting me. Now go!"

Garrick ran through the window. Nobody screamed at his presence. They couldn't see him. He followed the commotion in Kurai's wake to a stairwell and down to the basement.

How was he going to banish the Kitsune? She'd already proven herself a more skilled fighter. And now that she'd gone corporeal, she seemed even stronger. He couldn't even touch anything!

Garrick found Kurai in the server room and paused at the shredded doorway. What the hell was she doing?

Kurai was raging, wrenching server rack doors open before smashing the hardware within. It was like she was looking for something, her anger growing every time she didn't find it.

"Hey!" Garrick yelled, stalking forward, more bluster than confidence. He pointed with his scimitar, axe held low and ready. "You done worn out your welcome in Okinawa!"

Kurai glanced over her shoulder and rolled her eyes. "Go away," she said.

"Nuh-uh. That's my line!" Garrick edged forward, weapons ready.

Kurai ignored him and moved to the next server stack. She pulled the glass door completely off its hinges, throwing it to the floor. Glass shattered, and her gaze roved over the servers. She swore vilely and thrust a fist into the middle of the stack. Then she ripped a server free and flung it at Garrick. He flinched even though it couldn't touch him. The mangled computer passed through him and bounced off the shredded server stack to his right before crashing to the floor.

Garrick inched forward, not really looking forward to getting his ass handed to him again.

Kurai opened another server stack. A sudden smile bloomed on her face. "There it is!" Her head snapped toward Garrick, and he froze. Her eyes narrowed. "You've been a real pain in my ass. Perhaps it's time for you to know *real* pain. "She stepped toward him.

Garrick took an involuntary step back. "Uh, wha'd'ya mean? What'd you find there in that computer?"

"The way home. Most server farms connect to Hell. I just had to find the right server."

IT was connected to the underworld? No wonder Garrick hated computers! They really were infernal contraptions. He edged back, trying to keep his distance.

"Well then, git!" he said with more bravado in his voice than he felt on his face.

Kurai stalked forward, a cruel smile blossoming. "Oh, I'm going, but not because Basan banished me. I have more pressing commitments in Hell right now. And I could leave you behind, but you've officially pissed me off." Her wings flapped sharply in the tight aisle and then Kurai was on top of Garrick. Her hands clamped like manacles on his ghostly wrists, and she bore him to the ground.

Garrick struggled, kicking and flailing without effect. Kurai just smiled and stripped his weapons from his hands. She threw them disdainfully aside. "How did you ever become a ghost? You're the most pitifully weak spirit I've ever met." She grabbed Garrick's overalls and wrenched him to his feet. Then she flicked her free hand, and a dagger appeared in it. The dagger that had been buried in Basan's chest. She winked at Garrick, sheathed the dagger opposite its twin, and turned toward the server stack that connected to Hell.

Fear overwhelmed Garrick. He'd avoided Hell once and been chased out of Valhalla. He couldn't overpower Kurai. He had no tricks up his sleeve. Now he was doomed to an eternity of torments for the sin of challenging a Kitsune with anger issues. Garrick scrambled as she dragged him, trying to grab anything to stop his inexorable fate. Everything passed through his fingers.

What hurt most was that he'd never see Lilly again. He hoped she was in Valhalla, quaffing some good mead and giving that Ragnar fella the earful he deserved. Memories of Lilly's sharp tongue and sharper wit brought a sad smile, despite Garrick's panic. Yes, she'd do well in the Viking Longhouse.

Garrick's scrabbling fingers caught on a server stack's handle. He clutched it and jerked to a stop.

How? His gaze flicked to his corporeal hand.

Lilly. That was the second time today he'd thought of Lilly and turned corporeal. That was it. The secret to a ghost's powers.

Memories of the past. Normal ghosts were tormented souls with memories of pain and suffering; thus, the terror of haunted houses. But Garrick's memories of Lilly were of a life well-lived. Sorrow for his loss tinged with hope that their love would transcend this mortal realm. Garrick eyed his fingers wrapped around the server handle and thought of Lilly.

Power flowed into him. It crackled through his veins like lightning, a ghost's power to affect the mortal realm. The power to rattle the furniture, and maybe more. He looked at Kurai, who'd stopped in surprise when his hand caught the server. A small frown pinched her eyebrows.

Garrick pulled himself upright. "I said git, you varmint!" Then he raised his palms and the shredded bits of servers littering the aisle rose with them. A cloud of computer parts and broken glass hovered around him. He thrust his hands forward, and it all flew at Kurai like bullets. Or, in the case of the full server she'd thrown at him, flew like a tumbling box of metal.

Kurai released Garrick, stumbled back, and shifted from her corporeal form. The computer parts passed through her spirit and smashed into the open server door behind her. The glass door shattered. Kurai drew her daggers and snarled.

Garrick extended his palms and his cursed scimitar and Valhallan axe snapped into his hands. Oh, if Lilly could see him now!

He stepped forward, bits of glass crunching under his feet. Kurai launched at him in a flurry of attacks. She was still more skilled than him, but the balance of raw power had shifted to Garrick. Every block he made, every attack he swung, was so strong that Kurai's arms were flung aside like wet spaghetti.

Garrick stopped Kurai's advance cold. He forced her back toward the server. Her furious attacks became a furious defense. Then her back hit the server to Hell and—even though she wasn't corporeal—she stopped dead.

But she wasn't out of the fight yet. They both froze when Garrick's axe pressed against her neck just as her dagger pressed under his jaw. He couldn't see her second dagger but guessed it was poised to stab his gut. They were too close for his scimitar, so Garrick dropped it and clutched Kurai's arm. He grinned.

"Now, it looks like we got us a choice here." He glanced down at her wrist. "You stab me, and I'm draggin' you with me back to Valhalla. I'm okay with that, 'cause I'd see my Lilly again, even if they do make me a thrall for a thousand years. What kind of reception do you think you'll get the second time 'round?"

Kurai growled. Her gaze flicked to the axe against her neck.

"You ain't draggin' me to Hell, so here's the deal," Garrick said. "Instead of sendin' you back to that scarf rack in Chatan with this Valhallan blade and startin' the whole game of chase-the-demon again, I'm gonna let you go. I'd rather spend my vacation soakin' up the sun and drinkin' fruity cocktails." He pulled the axe away and stepped back. "Basan the fire-breathin' chicken said you're banished from these parts." He pointed to the server stack. "So, git, and never comeback."

Rage warred across Kurai's face, and for a moment Garrick thought she might attack him again, but instead, she spun and stepped into the server rack. The rack *shifted,* splitting open as she entered it to reveal an elevator that was entirely too big for the space it occupied. Kurai stepped inside, slammed her daggers back into their sheaths, and crossed her arms. Her gaze never left Garrick's as the server stack slid closed before her like a proper elevator door. Then the Kitsune was gone.

***

Garrick stretched out on the poolside lounger, reveling in the fabric's texture against his skin, and thought about Lilly. She would have loved Okinawa. The warm sun was edging toward sunset, hints of pink streaking the sky behind waving palm trees. The kids were back in the Hilton's pool, making a ruckus, while parents and businessmen ignored them. Garrick closed his corporeal eyes and basked.

A voice at his elbow made him crack an eyelid.

"You're a terrible ghost," Basan said. "Ghosts are supposed to haunt and terrify, not lounge by the pool."

Garrick grinned. "Nice to see you too." The rooster wasn't corporeal, which was probably smart. He would have been swarmed by children who didn't know better than to leave him alone. When Garrick had left Bridewell Incorporated, Basan had been gone. "Yer lookin' pretty good for taking the business end of Kurai's dagger."

The rooster snorted, ruffling his feathers. "Kurayami Kitsune—the dark fox—is a powerful spirit, but this is *my* territory. It'll take more than a cursed blade to put me down."

Another voice interrupted from Garrick's other side. A waitress leaned down with a coconut topped by a little pink umbrella. "Your Bahama Mama, sir."

"Why, thank ya kindly!" Garrick said. He took the drink, thinking about Lilly to make sure the rough coconut didn't slip through his fingers. It hurt a bit, thinking about her all the time so he could stay corporeal, but the memories were mostly good ones that made him smile.

As the waitress left, Basan said, "And how exactly do you plan to pay for that?"

"Well," Garrick said, stirring his drink with the straw, "I been thinkin' about that. Seein' as how I'm a ghost *and* a proper Viking who's visited Valhalla"—Basan's head snapped back at that, but Garrick wasn't gonna mention how he'd *left* Valhalla—"seems that drinkin' my drink and then fadin' into the ether is the only proper thing to do."

Basan's head cocked. "I suppose that makes sense for a ghost, but what does that have to do with being a Viking?"

"A bit of light thievery falls under the headin' of raids, which is the Viking way of life. It's our culture!"

"You're a farmer from Colorado," Basan said, deadpan.

"Shush now." Garrick waved at the rooster. Then he closed his eyes, took a long drink of the Bahama Mama, and smiled. "Oh, yeah. That's the ticket!" Strawberry, pineapple, and rum swirled on this tongue, cold enough to give him a headache.

The Speedo-clad businessman from yesterday strolled past with a towel over his shoulder, head swiveling as he looked for an available sun lounger. Garrick took another long pull on his Bahama Mama then set it down. He caught the businessman's gaze, smiled, and let himself fade into the ether.

The man shrieked and scrambled back. His foot slipped over the edge, and he tumbled into the pool.

No longer corporeal, Garrick chortled. He glanced at Basan, who gave the chicken head-bob version of rolling his eyes. Garrick stretched back out on the sun lounger but didn't re-corporate. He just basked in the sunset's dying rays and enjoyed the wonders of a ghost's afterlife, all the while thinking about Lilly.

*We authors like to think that we're in control of the stories we write. We aren't. Oh, sure, we plot and plan and try to give structure to the worlds we're building, but some characters have a bad habit of doing whatever the heck they want while we struggle to keep up. Garrick Thorsson is one of those characters. He was originally meant to be a red-shirt in the truest meaning of the term (if you're unfamiliar with the term red-shirt, ask any* Star Trek *fan). Garrick was supposed to die painfully in the novel* Death and the Taxman *as an object lesson to Grim of how horribly everything had gone wrong.*

*Garrick had other ideas.*

*He stole the scene, kicked a demon's ass, saved himself and Grim, and then sauntered away with a cocky grin. Sure, he was a ghost by that point, but he was going to make the best of it.*

*And I, the author, was left wondering what had just happened. It was amazing!*

*"Valhalla and Cocktails" is unique among the stories within* Grimsworld Tales *in that it takes place concurrently with one of the Grimsworld novels:* Death and the Dragon *(Book 2). If you wondered about the story icon of the dagger*

*inside the book, I recommend reading* Death and the Drag-on. *Kurai is so much more than she seems.*

*Garrick Thorsson will return in Book 3 of Grimsworld:* Death and the Immortal.

# LIGHT, LIES, AND LAST WORDS

BY BRITTANY RAINSDON

ABADDON'S ETERNAL DARKNESS GNAWED at my soul. After five millennia trapped in these wretched winding tunnels, I had given up wishing for the tiniest flicker of flame to light my way. It smelled of sulfur and smoke. Heat infused the air, and the unending darkness penetrated to my bones, suffocating all light along with my hope.

There could be no promise. No future. The realms beyond likely considered me dead—which meant there would be no rescue—even though I was very much alive.

I slid my hands along the rough stone walls, black angel wings flexing as I blindly navigated the twisting passages. Left here. Right. I counted my steps, shuffling forward as I raised my hand, feeling for the current of air above me. Another step forward and my wings ruffled against a boiling draft.

"You're close, Evelyn," I said to myself. Speaking out loud was one of the few ways I kept myself sane—one of the few ways I kept the *other* voices quiet.

I let go of the wall and flexed my wings, shooting upward as I counted to thirty, then down again for ten. The heat increased, hot wind whipping past me as I twisted around a corner and then landed. I felt fairly certain I'd retraced my steps correctly, to where I'd been held prisoner by Nigel.

Memories burned like a branding iron, but I iced them by reminding myself who I was.

"You are Evelyn, Captain of ten thousand Heavenly Hosts. Precious and favored angel of the Almighty—"

*Forgotten by the Almighty,* another voice seemed to say, even though I was alone. In the realm of eternal darkness, the walls vibrated and echoed back my greatest fears and regrets. Abaddon was built to torment.

"I am not forgotten." The words came out with a bitter bite and the echoes ceased.

I let out a breath and stepped forward cautiously until my knees hit something solid. My hands trembled as I leaned down to run them across the familiar grooves of the pillared altar I'd been tortured on by Nigel, the literal son of Satan.

But the rope wasn't there.

My stomach flipped as I slid my hand down and around, searching for the cursed cord that held me down during my torture, forcing me to remain corporeal so I could feel every slice against my flesh more poignantly.

I'd evaded Nigel and his dark army for centuries after we'd been trapped here. Eventually, they caught me. I had no idea how long they'd tortured me on that altar, indulging their anger, relishing their revenge on the only angel that had been trapped in Hell with them.

I shivered, skin crawling. "Once I find that rope, I'll do more than kill you, Nigel. I'll make you taste your own—"

My wrist hit something scratchy, and I shifted, finding a knot. My raw fingers unpicked the bit of rope, a feeling of vindication rising. But once it was free and I slid my hand down the cord, my chest tightened.

The rope had been cut.

I tested the length, wrapping the rope cautiously over my palms. There wasn't much, but enough remained that I could tie it around Nigel's wrist or ankle. Cautiously, I stowed the bit of rope and leapt back into the boiling current.

For the first time in five millennia, my heart fluttered with the spark of promise, and I imagined a future. A bitter smile broke across my lips as I realized I'd been wrong. The darkness in this hellhole had not suffocated *all* my hope.

Because I still hoped for revenge.

***

From what the demons I'd already destroyed had told me, Nigel had abandoned his private residence long ago. Still, the stink of Nigel's greasy hair lingered as I creaked open the roughly hewn door. Here, I intended to locate his most favored instruments of torture and make him taste the same pain he'd inflicted on me.

The walls were smoother here, carved by Cambion claws, and my footsteps echoed, suggesting the room to be a large one. I shuddered. The Cambion had been less than human, not quite demon, and pure abominations. As I slid my hands up, flexing my wings and following the wall's ridges upward, I imagined this chamber as a great room, tall enough a giant Nephilim could stand upright and not even scrape their boulder heads against the ceiling. But there were no hidden weapon caches higher up. I drifted back to the floor and swept my hands along the lower walls. Bits of torn fabric hung around the room. Halfway down the wall, a series of carved catches jutted out, dangling a dangerous display of knives. I let out a breath as my finger caught on the sharp barb of a nasty hook and I stumbled into another cache of weapons. They clattered against solid ground, echoing.

Memories of sizzling weapons slicing corporeal flesh flooded my mind. *No.* My throat closed as I folded my wings around myself, trembling, falling into a blur of memory. Of darkness and pain ripping—

I shook my head, focusing on another memory.

*"Stay true, Evelyn. You are precious in my sight."*

I wasn't even sure if the memory was real, but pinpricks spread across my body as the Almighty's last words burned within my soul. Real or imagined, my memory clung to the last moment I'd heard and felt His love. Archangel Gabriel had just left me on a balcony that overlooked the pearly gates. He'd conveyed our latest attack strategy against the rising demonspawn, but once the ten-foot double doors had snapped shut, a wave of fear crept over me. As I watched the heavenly troops gather below, I wondered how many would fall in the battle against giant Nephilim, Cambion, and demigods.

And then the Almighty's communication had come in a sudden flush.

I hadn't asked for confirmation of His care; I'd always felt confident that the Almighty loved me. In hindsight, I'm grateful such confirmations don't require asking. I needed those last words.

"I still do," I said out loud, voice shaking.

For it is the last words, the last moments in both Heaven and the mortal realm, that I relived over and over again. Gabriel's unrelenting attack orders. My subordinate, Alma's, confession of fear. My ex's cool touch of a single bony finger on my arm before the battle began.

I screamed and kicked the weapons away, feeling dirty and wrong for seeking the exact kind of evil I used to fight against.

*Does it even matter?*

*You aren't really an angel anymore.*

*They forgot you.*

I ignored the voices and focused on my memory of the Almighty as I tripped toward the wall, fumbling to find my way out. A third of the way down, my hands found something leathery and small nailed to the wall. At first, I imagined it was a coat or pocket, but as I traced the shape, my stomach twisted.

They were Cambion wings, dried and pressed like a trophy. Nigel's work.

*You killed the Cambion too, Evelyn.* The walls vibrated with my regret, sending painful memories searing with their sorrow and digging into the depths of my soul. I pressed my hands against my head, but this time I couldn't rid myself of the voices.

Because they were right.

The most honest creature I'd encountered in the last millennia was a male Cambion who had helped me escape Nigel. Back when I was imprisoned, the King of the Demigods had delighted in my daily torture. My only relief came at the end of his sessions, when he would bark at a servant to guard me. One day after Nigel had finished, a sniffling creature approached the platform and introduced himself as Garith. The Cambion had promised he would untie my bonds and return my sword, *Mercy*, if I promised I'd unmake him and end his suffering. For such is life in the depths of Abaddon.

I'd agreed.

Once we were finally free of Nigel and I felt as safe as one can in Abaddon, I'd kept my promise. As I sliced my blade through Gareth's middle, he'd gasped. Then he was gone. For *Mercy* grants a true death, unmaking an immortal soul. Forever.

In the millennia after, I'd sometimes imagine what Gareth had looked like. I could tell he had been smaller than most of the other demonspawn, with flimsy leather wings and a short tail. I didn't regret unmaking him. It had been a mercy to do so. But whenever I relived the memory, I found myself imagining alternate endings. Ones where I wasn't alone, where for one brief moment, I had a friend in Hell.

Since then, I'd hunted every demon, Cambion, Nephilim, and demigod in Abaddon's halls, granting them a clean death of unmaking. I vowed that even if I never escaped Abaddon, so-help-me, not a single creature of darkness would escape me.

I pulled away from the wall and pried myself from the past. "Nigel will answer for what he's done," I said out loud. "To you … and to me."

"So, you are open to talking then?" Nigel's haughty voice echoed from behind and I whirled around, unsheathing my sword. The leathery Cambion wings fell to the ground.

How long had he been here?

"Because talking to yourself, well, that isn't a good sign." His voice came from above. He was using the unnatural nature of the tunnels to confuse.

I shifted, focusing on his words and smell. "I've unmade your demons." I took a breath and listened carefully, noting the echoes bouncing. "The Nephilim are gone forever, as are your demigods and Cambion."

"But not me." I heard the smile in his voice. "Is it possible you have a soft spot? Becau—"

Something shifted over my head, and my wings snapped to attention. I didn't hear what else he had to say as I rocketed upward—and smacked against the ceiling. Pain sparked against the back of my head, and I slunk back, shifting to spirit form. How had the ceiling moved and where was he hiding? The stupid demigod didn't have wings like me. He couldn't just float...

"Come out and face me, Nigel!"

He didn't respond.

I cursed. But then there was the creak of something moving—a door in the ceiling! I flared my wings, following Nigel as I phased through the door and into the twisting maze of tunnels that peppered the deepest level of Hell. I could sense him ahead as a hot current whipped past me. Brittle feathers broke from my wingtips as I rematerialized. I imagined their dark tufts floating away, molting as I twisted through the air.

The tunnel leveled and I landed awkwardly, feeling with one hand along the rough walls as I tightened my grip on *Mercy*. Heat pulsed against my palm like a heartbeat. Had I lost him?

I held my breath.

After what felt like a century, a rock clattered and I pivoted, slicing. My blade clanged against another—his cursed sword.

"Evelyn, stop!" Nigel groaned as he pushed against the weight of my weapon, but a wave of energy and power flowed through me as I pressed forward.

But then my blade slipped.

I gasped as he kicked me in the stomach. Stumbling, I hugged my chest.

"Evelyn," Nigel growled. "You *must* listen to me. "His voice was laced with annoyance, as though he were a parent reprimanding a child.

I ignored him and lunged again, swinging *Mercy*, but this time I only caught air. He must have shifted sideways.

"I waited for you. I *let* you find me"—he grunted again—"because we must talk."

"If you let me find you, you made a poor decision." I sliced again, and this time his blade caught mine.

"Please, Evelyn..." He pushed against my volley, voice tight. But he was losing. I pressed closer, gaining, as he cried, "Evelyn! I know the way out!"

The sureness in his voice made me waver. Suddenly, he shoved and I fell to my knees.

*Kill him.*

*Unmake him.*

*He lies!*

The words sizzled against my mind as I scrambled to my feet. But *his* words had taken root, and my mind was rushing to catch up with the glimmer of hope he had planted in my heart.

"If you know the way out, why are you still here?" I shouted. My voice echoed above and around me, twisting back morphed.

I closed my eyes, focusing on the sounds. Fear, regret, and anger vibrated back, choking out the impossible suggestion of escape. Hell's lowest level had no food, no water, no comfort, no light. It was eternal misery. I'd already accepted eternity in Abaddon. Once Nigel was unmade, I'd shift to spirit form and drift as best I could.

But if there was a way out ... I ruffled my wing feathers. "You're a liar, Nigel."

"I can prove it." Nigel's voice came from the right and I jerked toward him, raising my sword.

But there was a strange grating, *click-click* noise, and then a spark.

Something flickered.

I winced, eyes watery with pain, as a small flame danced in Nigel's hand. The demon's dark eyes met mine as for the first time I saw our conditions. The craggy floor and ceiling looked like a monster's mouth with broken teeth. Some of the stalactites swayed as if the tunnels were alive and breathing. Nigel ran his free hand through matted hair, giving a slippery smile before darkness overwhelmed and the flame was extinguished.

My knees buckled. I gripped the wall for strength. "How did you do that?"

"I've been picking at the wall." Nigel spoke slowly, voice tight. "I've picked and chipped and scraped for Hell knows how long. A thousand years, maybe? But my patience has paid off because I finally made a hole. It's barely big enough to fit my hand through, and when I reached outside, I found *this*."

"That's impossible." I shook my head. "You used magic to trick me or—"

"Swear on the Almighty you won't harm me, and I'll let you try it yourself."

My stomach twisted. *Stay true, Evelyn.* The Almighty's words rang through my mind—but what was I to be true to now? I swallowed and swore. "I won't harm you, Nigel ... for now."

He stepped forward and shoved something small against my palm. The object was rectangular, smooth, light, and there was a rough-feeling wheeled mechanism at the top. I tested the mechanism, recreating the click-clicky sound. Nothing happened. I tried again and this time a flame burst in my hand.

I dropped the strange thing, and it clattered on the ground, the world dark again.

The air shifted as I sensed Nigel sinking to the ground to retrieve the object. My fingers itched on my blade. Another part of me remembered the rope and my plans for a more fitting revenge.

But that wasn't me.

It *couldn't* be me.

"I know what you want." Nigel's voice remained soft as he straightened himself. "But I propose we both put our hatred aside. We need each other."

"I don't need you."

"You do if you want to find the way." He cleared his throat. "And I can't make it out without your help either. That's why I waited here for you. *Mercy* may not be able to open the gates of Abaddon, but it's one of the three great blades. If my weapon can make a chip, yours should be able to make a gouge."

"Should?"

"I'm hopeful. I've seen light, Evelyn. I've felt the sun. It's a different kind of warmth, if you remember…" He paused. "But the choice is yours. Unmake me and risk being stuck in Abaddon for eternity. Or partner with me and remember what it is like to live."

Silence stretched between us. Hope plucked at my soul. "May the Almighty forgive me," I whispered. I sheathed *Mercy* and made my deal with the devil.

***

Nigel refused to take me to his hole until I took an oath on the Almighty that I'd grant him safe passage through the widened crack—and that I'd let him escape first. Nigel then made a similar oath in Lucifer's name, but somehow his oath didn't ring with the same level of conviction as mine.

As we wound through the pitch, Nigel talked as if we were old friends. I mostly grunted in reply, but Nigel was more than capable of carrying a conversation on his own. He asked questions I had no intention of answering until finally my upper lip curled into a snarl. "Once we're out of here, our truce is over. Don't get comfortable."

"I expected as much."

He shifted, directing me down a more temperate draft, and I followed in silence. Nigel couldn't seem to stand that. "But you're not the only one who was abandoned here, Evelyn. We're more alike than you care to admit. My father—"

"Has nothing to do with me."

"I've felt your fears, Evelyn. They vibrate in the walls, just like mine. Only I've heard yours spoken directly. You used to scream them in my chambers. You hated Gabriel and even the Almig—"

"I never cursed the Almighty."

"No?" He directed me up and around a tall pillar, tracing a hand on rough stone. "Just like I never cursed my father. Lucifer left me to rot. I'm his son."

I ruffled my wing feathers, keeping my voice cold. "I don't feel bad for you."

"I'm not asking you to. But I'm asking you to understand. We've both been left behind by those we trusted and now—"

"Don't compare me to you."

He gave a bitter laugh. "Oh, you're worried about what the other angels will think? Once they hear of your deal with a devil? I'd have thought you wouldn't care. You did, after all, love that traitor, Grim."

I stiffened as hot venom, a deep hatred rivaling that of Nigel's, burned within. "Don't pretend to know him."

"Come on, Evelyn. Everyone knows Death."

*But not everyone gets to know Grim.*

Or at least the Angel Grim I had known before he fell from grace and had been stripped of his wings to become Death. I closed my eyes, remembering our late-night flights during the dawn of creation. I'd buried my face in his tan feathers and stared into perfect amber eyes.

I had loved him.

Even after his familiar features were gone, even when the Almighty had transformed him into the infamous Grim Reaper, I had loved Grim. Because Grim was still Grim.

At least, I'd *thought* he was.

Nigel shifted beside me, closer than before. "I wasn't there that day, when he lost his wings and his flesh melted away. Did you wonder if he'd be able to *feel* anymore? Or if rotting into a corpse had made him incapable of love?"

I shook my head "You don't know—"

"I suppose him sealing us *both* in Abaddon answers that question. He had to know what we'd do to you and…"

A hand brushed mine, reaching for *Mercy*. Instinctively, I flared my wings, knocking Nigel sideways as I drew my weapon. Nigel scrambled against the rock, and suddenly I realized why Nigel was so close, distracting me with talk of my ex.

My voice darkened. "You lied, Nigel."

"I didn't lie. I'm not *hurting* you. "His voice was matter of fact. "And after I carved my way out of here, you would still be free to follow… once you found my hole."

My grip on *Mercy* tightened. So that was it. Nigel needed my sword, not me. But *I* couldn't escape without *him*. Frustration welled within my chest. How could I trust a snake that had settled itself in my back pocket … my back pocket! I fished out the scrap of rope. "New deal. You're going corporeal until we surface, Nigel."

He laughed. "Why would I do that?"

"So I can better sense your movements, and you can't sneak up on me again."

"And you'll just trust me to '*stay corporeal*?'"

"No. I have your torture rope." I flung the cord at him. "Tie it around your ankle."

"Great." Nigel fumbled. "*This* will make you feel better?"

"Along with your sword." I nodded even though he couldn't see me. "Give it here."

"No." His voice dipped. "I'd be defenseless. You have *Mercy.*"

I shook my head. "I'll be too busy widening the crack to fight. Which means I'll be the defenseless one." Nigel sputtered but I raised my voice. "So, you *will* give me your sword, or we part ways right now."

"But you'll be trapped here!"

I tried to make my voice come out strong, but my knees went weak. "I've had plenty of time to make peace with that fate."

Nigel paused. Then there was a bright ring as he unsheathed his blade. "Fine. If it makes you feel better."

I sheathed his blade under my belt, pretending that it did.

But if I was honest with myself, nothing would make me feel better.

***

I smelled the mortal realm before I saw it. A sweet scent carried on a spiraling spurt of air. And once I spotted the slit of light dancing in the distance, I flew to the opening in the ceiling and pressed my face against the crack. A cool warmth breathed against my cheek as sunlight dazzled my eyes. I blinked fiercely, unable to see because I'd been in darkness so long. There were strange sounds outside, a whizzing and whooshing sound followed by strange honking that definitely was not from a goose.

My brow knit with confusion as I pulled away. "Megiddo is a city now?" It had been a desert valley when Grim had opened the gates of Abaddon.

Nigel shook his head. "This crack didn't open into Megiddo. I'm not sure where the city is but look at the side of that metal rubbish bin on wheels. It says, 'City of New Orleans.'"

I peeked back at the crack, eyeing the bin.

"Careful. Being by the rubbish is great and all, especially when the humans leave out interesting artifacts but ... sometimes it leaks."

As if on cue, something slimy dripped down the crack, smelling a bit *too* sweet. Like overripe fruit. I pulled away, frowning. But in truth, I didn't care if the crack spilled us into a literal lake of lava, so long as we could get out.

"What's all this?" I said, noticing the foreign objects he'd pulled inside the rift.

"Mortal trash." There were scraps of crumbled paper that he claimed were newspapers, along with scavenged clothing, fruit rinds, and a tin can with sharp edges. It smelled like spoiled fish.

"Why'd you take that?" I balanced the can on the tip of my sword and held it towards him.

Nigel winced and shoved it away, face turning blotchy. "I—I hadn't eaten in five millennia..." His voice broke as he turned away. "I may be immortal, but unlike you, I'm still half-human. You try avoiding food after an eternity of twisting hunger."

I dropped the can and took a step forward, inspecting the demigod. He was still head and shoulders taller than me; but with matted hair and skin smeared with dirt, he looked nothing like the regal prince of darkness I remembered from the mortal realm. His haughty, proud aura had changed, making him seem ... broken.

Something twisted in my gut. Could the suffering of Abaddon have had a positive effect on Nigel? Could he have changed? Was it possible?

For a brief moment, I considered asking Nigel to look at me. The eyes are the window to the soul, and maybe through them I could see the light of hope burning inside him, or a change of heart, or a thirst for redemption.

But I didn't dare look.

I turned and shook my head, approaching the crack with *Mercy*. If Nigel allowed me to see into his soul, he'd see into mine as well. I wouldn't risk it.

Because I was too terrified to know the state of mine.

***

A day later, the cat came. Shabby and gray, the creature looked to have missed more than a few meals. Still, the sight of it made my heart nearly explode. Cats weren't bound to the mortal realm like humans. A kitty could slip into Hell with us—or just as easily access Heaven and paw-deliver a message to Gabriel—maybe even the Almighty Himself.

It leaned around the rubbish bin, rubbing its body and purring. "Here kitty!" My attempt at a sing-song voice came out as a growl, and the cat stopped.

I poked my dirt-covered arm through the crack and bent awkwardly so I could watch the cat's reaction. One ear cocked sideways, but it wasn't enticed. Cats are selfish creatures, motivated by self-preservation and food. If I could bribe it...

"Nigel!" I kicked the demigod awake and motioned for him to help me. "Are you hiding more food?"

His brow knit. "Why?"

"There's a cat!" I hissed. "If we convince it to help us—"

Rubble crunched as Nigel climbed to his feet. He grubbed around some papers, tossing bits of mortal trash this way and that, but instead handing me anything, he elbowed me aside.

"She won't like you," I said as I blocked him, but he nodded at the kitty.

"I have a better chance. That's a familiar. Witch's cat." He pointed. "See that crescent patch?"

"No," I said. But I did, so I let him pass.

"Here kitty!" He shoved part of his arm up through the hole—he couldn't fit quite as far as me—wriggling whatever offering he'd brought. "There, that's right." I heard the cat purr as Nigel continued. "If you help us, we'll—"

There was a loud smack followed by an explosive *hiss!* Nigel dropped from the hole. He stared at his hand as if it had been mangled. "That feral, maggot-infested—"

I shoved past Nigel, but as I craned my neck to see through the hole, it was obvious; the cat had vanished. "What did you do to it?"

"IT PEED ON ME!" Nigel frantically patted his wet arm with crumbled papers. "Stupid litt—"

"Must've been marking his territory." My lips twitched.

"Shut up."

"Oh, that sounds prophetic!" A long-forgotten sensation rose up my chest. "Furry little beast marks the son of Satan. Intrepid warrior." I saluted the kitty with a smile.

It was the only time I laughed in Abaddon.

***

Four days later, after the dust and rock chips had settled against my feet, the hole to the mortal realm was wide enough to squeeze through. At least it was wide enough for *me* to squeeze through. Nigel would struggle near the top. And that was precisely the point.

I had a plan.

Moonlight streamed through the hole, casting strange shadows across Nigel's face as he rested amongst the rubble, sleeping. With a nudge, I shook him awake.

He glanced from me to the hole and grinned. "Good work, Evelyn." He dusted off his knees and stood. "Did you want me to take a turn swinging?"

"No." I frowned. "You will never touch *Mercy*. It's finished."

Nigel's forehead creased as he motioned above. "But that isn't—"

"It's wide enough. You'll fit. I'm not obligated to make it easy."

Nigel raised an eyebrow, looking to the opening as if calculating. He stretched his shoulders. "Fine. But I need my blade back. Once we're in the mortal realm, I know you'll try to unmake me."

I ruffled my wing feathers. "I keep my promises, Nigel, but I never promised to return your blade."

Nigel's face reddened.

"You can have your head start." I motioned at the hole. "Like I promised."

Nigel's upper lip curled as he moved away from me. "Fine. But I don't need a blade to get what I want. Remember that."

I folded my wings around my shoulders as he scaled the short wall, bracing himself against the rock. He moved deftly, and for a moment, I wondered if I had miscalculated Nigel's size. But then he stopped. His large shoulders wiggled helplessly against the rock as he kicked to propel himself forward. He moved an inch. Then none. His feet dangled.

I imagined how he looked on the other side. With that rope on, he would still be corporeal, which meant any mortal would see a dirty, overgrown man sprouting from the ground.

Perfect.

Before we'd been trapped in Abaddon, every city had boasted a contingent of guardian angels who watched over the faithful. Surely New Orleans had a party that would come by soon. I may have promised not to hurt Nigel during our escape, but I didn't promise to help him evade capture. And a corporeal half-Nigel should certainly make enough of a ruckus that—

Nigel groaned. "Help me back down so you can widen this."

"No." I gritted my teeth. I'd hold him in place for the next hour if I had to.

"But Evelyn—"

"You just have to suck in."

Suddenly Nigel stopped flailing, and his voice went muffled. I heard the words 'that's it,' and 'keep pulling!'

Ice knotted my stomach. If he was talking that way, it wasn't a patrol angel who'd found him. Nigel braced his feet against the wall, pushing, and this time he moved forward. I reached for his legs grabbing at his ankle, but he kicked and smacked me in the teeth.

I fell back. Bits of unsettled rock pelted my skin and wings while Nigel slipped through the surface.

No!

Seeing stars, I stumbled to get up.

But it was too late.

I took a running leap into the light and pumped my wings, then folded them close. I phased, focusing my willpower to change my visage to appear mortal as I surfaced. Whatever human was helping Nigel wouldn't be prepared for an angel.

I shot from the hole like a rock from a slingshot, but I was hardly through the surface when something solid and hard rammed me in the chest.

Breath kicked out of me as I smacked into a brick wall opposite the dumpster. Part of the wall crumbled around me. Dazed, I ruffled my wings, shaking off dust and glass and bits of brick rubble. My illusion fizzled as I struggled to focus my eyes. I mumbled something about liars, expecting to see Nigel, but instead a four-legged beast stood over me, looking nothing like the demigod I'd just spoken with.

I shook my head. An enormous cow, with horns the size of tree trunks jutting out of its head and fiery red eyes, pawed at the ground.

Demonspawn.

"Hurry!" Nigel roared from somewhere behind. I rolled to my side. Shards of glass and bits of rubble bit my skin as I scrambled aside.

The beast snarled, smoke curling from its nostrils.

"The swords!" Nigel yelled.

The demon-cow's hooves stamped near my head as it shoved its wet muzzle against my waist, digging at *Mercy*. I snatched the blade away, but the beast's muzzle opened, revealing pointed teeth, which bit down on the handle of Nigel's sword.

"Hey!" I yelled, kicking at its legs. I swiped *Mercy*, but before I could make contact, the demonic creature bucked sideways. Nigel's sword dangled from its mouth, and it gave another muffled snarl. Its tail flicked as it trotted twenty feet back down the alley to where Nigel waited, picking the rope off his ankle.

Above us, a window suddenly brightened with light. Great. We'd woken at least one mortal.

I shifted, no longer corporeal, and glanced behind my back at the hole I'd just made with my shoulder. Heavens that hurt! At least no one appeared to be living in *that* section of the building. Overturned boxes littered the floor, along with broken bits of mortal inventions I had no name for. Hopefully it was just a storage room.

I faced Nigel, crouched for battle.

The demon-cow snorted as it lowered its head, then dropped the slippery blade. Carefully Nigel picked up the sword and wiped away the saliva using his dirty tunic. He scratched the creature's ears.

"Evelyn, meet Molly. Distant spawn of Moloch."

Molly lifted her head, eyeing me with round red eyes.

My upper lip curled. "Where'd you get that?"

"The stray cat. I bribed her to hunt down a demon for a half-tin of week-old tuna. It chose Molly, probably hoping I'd get it some cream. If that fursplat didn't pee on me, I probably would've obliged."

My chest tightened. Nigel *had* planned this escape with more precision than I could have realized. "I'm taking you to Gabriel," I said, but my voice shook.

"Really?" Nigel raised an eyebrow. "I have no intention of being judged by Gabriel or the Almighty or whoever is in charge up there now. If you chase me, I'll fight. But if you leave me alone, I'll leave in peace."

My heart pounded wildly against my ribs, but I widened my stance, planting my feet. "I cannot release you into the world."

"You already have. Don't make others suffer more for it. I won't ask again. Walk. Away."

But I lunged.

Nigel slapped Molly hard on the behind.

Before I could reach them, the cow bucked and opened her maw. Flames surged from her mouth. I ducked behind a pile of rubble and folded my wings around myself as the crumbled bricks became bright embers. Eventually the heat ebbed, and smoke swirled around me.

But behind me, there was the telltale snap and sizzle of a fire. The storage room had burst into flames.

"Their blood will be on your hands, Evelyn," Nigel called. "You can chase me, but so many mortals are sleeping…"

Panic rose up my throat as I glanced up at the windows. All were dark, save the one. Suddenly the bright one swooshed open and a black woman in a nightcap leaned out the window. "What in the hell—Marv! Marv, I think there was a gas explosion." She moved away from the window, voice shrill. "Marv, get up! There's a fire!"

She couldn't see me—no mortal could, unless their third eye had been opened—but she could definitely see the rubble and flames licking up the side wall. The fire was spreading fast.

Nigel watched me, one hand on Molly.

I hesitated. If I didn't go after Nigel now, I didn't know when I'd be able to track him again. But if the fire spread…

"Fight me or save the mortals."

*Almighty, help me.* I sent up a desperate prayer but was met with the usual silence. I couldn't wait for an answer. Cursing, I flexed my wings and swooped into the air.

Nigel ran as I began knocking on windows, shattering some, leaving no one behind. Over the next few minutes, humans poured into the street, waking their friends, their eyes wide with fear as they watched the large building burn. Strange carriages arrived—fire trucks, I heard someone say—with flashing lights and roaring sirens. Brave mortals unpacked flexible tubes that poured water over the flames.

I turned corporeal again to help a few lingering mortals down the stairs. Then I shifted to the back of the crowd, folding my wings protectively around myself and watching them work. Sour guilt slipped up my throat.

It was my fault.

This was my fault.

*It's not.* A familiar presence warmed my heart, so quiet that at first, I didn't hear it clearly. But as I focused, the Almighty's voice grew stronger.

*It's not your fault. But you must hurry. Not everyone is out, Evelyn. Move. NOW!*

Without thinking, I snapped back into the air. Images poured into my heart of a small family huddled in a corner, unable to escape. The visual morphed, and I saw a window with spider-vein cracks. Following the guidance of the Almighty, I found the window and swooped, catapulting through.

Once inside, smoke smothered as the muffled fire only a floor below popped and sizzled.

"Hello?" I called, but nothing could be heard over the roar of the flames. I moved down a hallway and turned right, then phased, turning corporeal so the family could see and hear me. "Hello!"

"Here!" a voice called, retching.

I followed the voice and kicked open a door, finding them huddled, just like the picture the Almighty placed in my heart. Father, mother, child.

Blindly, the man reached for me, pulling his wife up. She cradled a toddler, whose face and body had been wrapped in damp blankets. My heart hitched.

The child wasn't moving.

I pulled one of each of the parents' arms over my shoulders. "The exit is this way!" We struggled forward halfway down the hall, but suddenly the woman collapsed, nearly dropping her daughter.

"Erica? Elizabeth?" the man cried.

I tried to carry her, carry him, but it was impossible. I couldn't shoulder all three of them and—

The man fell to his knees. Sweat plastered his hair and clothing to his skin as he shook his wife. "Erica!" But the woman had lost consciousness. Suddenly he grabbed the baby and shoved it into my arms. "Get her out. Now! Keep her safe." He choked, pulling at his wife.

"But you—"

"We'll only slow you down"—he coughed—"and I'm not leaving my wife. Save my daughter. I'll follow."

"But—"

*You have to go, Evelyn.* The Almighty's voice twisted the knot in my gut.

"I—I'll come back," I whispered, clutching the girl.

The man didn't answer.

Heat blazed and smoke stung as I shuffled down the hall. Glass tinkled underfoot as I leapt over the upturned furniture and landed on the window ledge. Curling my wings protectively around the girl, I jumped into the night.

Smoke billowed around us, shielding us from onlookers as I flared my wings and coasted to the ground. We landed behind a fresh pile of rubble. As I phased, appearing mortal again, the blanket fell from the girl's face, revealing chubby cheeks and tight curls. My heart clenched.

She was so small, I guessed maybe three years old.

"Over here!" I yelled, waving my arms at a pair of medics that were checking out a shaken-looking elderly woman in the back of one of their flashing carriages. "I have a little girl."

Suddenly, the child moved, kicking. Hope rippled through me. She was alive. But her parents—

One of the medics took the girl from my arms while the other began a barrage of questions, attempting to shepherd me to their carriage. "What's her name? Does she have allergies? Any medical conditions? What about you?"

But before the medics got an answer, I shifted back into spirit form and headed for the flames.

When I returned through the spider-veined window, I found the couple collapsed beside the overturned couch. They were holding hands, heads tilted against each other. In spite of the shiny red burns and blotchy patches of ash smeared on their clothes and skin, they were the picture of peace.

But their souls were gone.

Cold pitted in my stomach as the flames roared behind. Something snapped. Ten feet away, the floorboards collapsed and a hole expanded, rippling towards me. At the last second, I stretched open my wings and flew from the window.

Behind me, the room exploded.

A sob escaped my throat. Where could I go?

I headed back to the hole in Abaddon, part of me wishing I'd never left it. Yet once I landed, I was transfixed by the carnage. Eventually, the medics bundled the last few survivors into their flashing carriages and drove away. Firefighters in black and yellow uniforms attacked the blaze with hoses, while others directed mortals from the scene. There was noise, so much noise, and even though I'd escaped Abaddon, I could still feel the walls branding me with shame.

*Liar.*

*Murderer.*

*Their blood is on your hands.*

Someone squeezed my shoulder, and I jumped.

"It's been a long time, Evelyn."

I looked up, gritty tears streaming down my face, as the Archangel Gabriel pulled me up and into his arms.

***

Gabriel took me to Heaven.

As we walked through the familiar halls of the palace of angels, striding past the stained-glass windows, whispers and furtive glances peppered my back. My cheeks heated.

I knew I looked different.

My once-gleaming white armor was nearly black, stained from the horrors of Abaddon. My dark hair was now tangled and dirty. Scars dotted my skin. But I was home and none of that should have mattered.

I was supposed to feel peace, I was supposed to feel warmth.

Someone laughed as we walked by, and I narrowed my eyes, shooting daggers at them. The laughter stopped.

No, I didn't feel warmth. I felt anger. Shame. And more than anything else, an enormous wave of guilt.

I had thought I could outsmart Nigel, but he had escaped. In a moment of desperation and weakness, I had

221

released the last demigod into the mortal realm. His merciless attack on the innocent proved he had never changed. I had been foolish to believe he could. Failing to capture Nigel today had put hundreds of mortals at risk. If he wasn't captured soon, countless more would suffer. I needed to make this right.

I hated him.

I hated him so much!

The whispers were finally silenced after Gabriel led me out onto the upper balcony and closed the ten-foot-tall double-doors. I recognized the marble balcony from my memories. It had been one of my favorite spots five millennia ago—that's how long Gabriel claimed I'd been gone.

But Heaven had changed. The scent of cherry blossoms still infused the air, shimmery phoenixes still rose against misty clouds, and the hum of music played in the distance ... but the music had morphed into something Gabriel called Rock and Roll. He also referenced a holy bureaucracy with rules and nuances I no longer understood. There were even machines and inventions invading the halls, like the zooming circular creation that had caught itself on the oriental rug just outside the balcony. Gabriel had called it a *blessed broomba*. Gotta keep Heaven clean.

"Evelyn?" Gabriel motioned for me to sit on the bench overlooking the edge of Heaven and the glistening pearly gates. "Can you tell me what happened?"

I shook my head and curled my wings protectively around myself. I was no longer used to sitting.

"I already told you, Nigel—"

"Not about Nigel. About you."

I swallowed, hesitating.

But eventually I told him everything. Most everything, anyway. "...so, you see, we have to do something."

Gabriel's face creased with concern as he stared across Heaven. Below us, at the pearly gates, hopeful souls waited, milling about in standard issue white robes.

"Gabriel, you understand, don't you?"

"Yes." He sighed and finally turned to face me.

"Then you know I have to fix it." My voice cracked. "I must address this with the Almighty."

"You addressed it in prayer. The Almighty won't invite you to speak directly in his presence. Even before your ... imprisonment ... you know how rare that was."

"But I—I need to explain." My voice trembled.

Gabriel touched my arm and motioned again for me to sit. "You've been through much."

I nodded and finally complied. The cool stone was an unfamiliar relief.

"We will do what we can to mitigate the situation, and I'm sure eventually He w—"

"Eventually?" My eyebrows shot skyward. "Has the Almighty changed that much in my absence? Does he no longer car—"

"The Almighty does not change." Gabriel lowered his voice, eyes tracing my dirty uniform. "But the unclean burn in His presence. It's why mortals are sent to Purgatory, for a final cleansing. In your current state—"

"You're worried about how I'm dressed?" My lips trembled as I gestured at my armor. "This armor is stained from millennia of unimaginable torture. What do you expect? Once I get fresh clothes and—"

"It isn't your armor that concerns me."

His words had a bite to them. Abaddon had changed me. Before I'd had righteous anger and holy conviction, but now, I harbored a cruelty and a hatred I'd not known could exist in angels. Was this how the fallen became demons? I hugged my chest. "So, you intend to send me to Purgatory? To cleanse me?"

"No." Gabriel grimaced. "The Almighty wishes you to take a special assignment."

I straightened. "I'm ready to prove myself again. I unmade all the hellspawn in Abad—"

Gabriel held up a hand. "I do not question your talents on the battlefield: however, you cannot serve as captain, Evelyn."

My face fell.

"You will be a guardian angel."

I stood, fury rising within. "I'm a warrior, not some city watch or a babysitter."

Gabriel frowned, and he motioned for me to sit again. "At least listen."

I stared at Gabriel for a moment but finally lowered back to the bench.

Gabriel fumbled with his robes and pulled out a picture attached to a scroll. "Your charge, should you accept, is an orphan. Death just collected her parents' souls a few hours ago. She's alone in the world."

Gabriel handed me the picture, and my heart went cold. It was the little girl I'd pulled from the fire. The paper creased, and my hands shook as I read her information.

Elizabeth Kolnik.

I had been right. She was only three.

Gabriel's voice went muffled as he kept talking, and I didn't hear the rest. As I stared at the little girl's face, darkness flooded my soul and chilling voices echoed in my head, as if Abaddon had somehow clung to me.

*You're the reason that girl's parents are dead.*

*The reason she's alone.*

*Murderer.*

I closed my eyes. If I hadn't tried to escape Abaddon, if I'd accepted my fate and endured, or if I'd just been smart enough to trick Nigel instead of falling into his traps...

*Stop, Evelyn.*

A heat ripped through me.

*You are still precious in my sight.*

The memory of the Almighty's last words seared with comforting heat, the same as they did whenever my mind had been warped by the voices of Abaddon.

But in spite of the warmth, I cried out in my mind.

*"Then why did you abandon me!"*

Heat pulsated as new words flowed into my heart.

*I sent you light.*

In my mind, I saw the crack and recalled the sweet relief as my face pressed against the rock.

*You suffered to advance my Plan, to end the Nephilim.*

My fingers gripped Mercy's hilt. He'd known I would hunt them down.

But my eyes misted as I opened them and saw the little girl. Her eyes pierced through the photograph.

*She is precious, too.*

A feeling came with the words, a powerful sense that this little girl was also part of His Plan. Then the Almighty's voice faded, and the warmth ebbed, but I knew—just as I did five millennia ago—how much He loved me. And how much the Almighty loved *her*.

Gabriel was still talking, but as I clutched the photo, I cut him off. "I accept the post."

I didn't need to hear anything else.

***

Hours later, clean and dressed in fresh armor—midnight black armor—I stood guard over a hospital crib in the mortal realm. Little Elizabeth sucked her thumb, exhausted, but no longer alone as she slept. Doctors and nurses buzzed just outside her room while someone called a 'social worker' rested on the couch.

Elizabeth Kolnik wasn't out of the woods, but I could tell my ex wouldn't be visiting her any time soon. If Grim tried anything, I'd rip his teeth out.

Carefully, I reached through the metal crib bars and touched Elizabeth's soft hair, fingers fading through a mess of thick curls. "You are loved, little Elizabeth," I whispered. "You are precious, indeed."

The child would never hear me, but I would tell her how precious she was every day. I would honor her father's last request to keep her safe. And even though she couldn't feel me, I would always find a way to show her the light.

Just as the Almighty had done for me.

*I was absolutely thrilled when award-winning author Brittany Rainsdon agreed to write "Light, Lies, and Last Words" for* Grimsworld Tales. *Brittany is a fellow Writers of the Future winner, and she's known for writing kick-ass leading ladies and heart-wrenching stories that leave you cheering. She's also among the mere handful of authors who have appeared in TWO volumes of Writers of the Future (Volumes 37 and 38), once as a published finalist and then again as a winner.*

*I wanted to write Evelyn's origin story for quite some time, and I tried to, I really did. Yet, no matter how hard I tried, it never came out right. My stories are light and fun and Evelyn's tale isn't exactly a happy one. It needed a more deft hand than mine, and I could think of no one better than Brittany Rainsdon. So, I handed Evelyn's origin story to Brittany with the trepidation of a parent handing over their firstborn child.*

*I needn't have feared. Brittany wove a tale that did Evelyn proud. "Light, Lies, and Last Words" is the perfect blend of sad and hopeful that is Brittany's hallmark. I couldn't have been happier.*

*You can find more of Brittany Rainsdon's stories at https://rainsdonwrites.com/*

*Evelyn and Elizabeth with return in Book 3 of Grimsworld:* Death and the Immortal.

# The Grim Reaper's Game

When I reap a soul, I fully expect them to complain about it. Nobody likes dying, but when the Grim Reaper calls, you have no choice but to answer.

Brenda Agonos refused to answer the call.

My metaphor falls apart here, but the point remains. Brenda was being a pain in my scythe. I eyed the septuagenarian sitting on her hospital bed.

"'No' is not an option," I intoned. "I will happily listen to any deathbed confessions you may have, but your time in your mortal coil has passed."

"No," she said again, looking rather smug, I might add. "I'm not dying today. Too much to do. Now get out of my way."

I scrubbed at my skull with bony fingers. Why did the deceased have to be so belligerent? It's simple. You live, you die, your soul moves on to its final destination. I don't care if people go to Heaven or Hell or get stuck somewhere in between. My job is simply to ease their passing.

"Very well. If you have no confession, then I wish you the best in the afterlife." I swung my scythe through her body.

Nothing happened.

That wasn't right. My scythe should have cut her soul free, a painless transition to the afterlife. I swung again. Brenda's soul obstinately stayed inside her body. I eyed her smug wrinkled face. The black stare of Death's eyeless skull usually withers any soul's resistance, but Brenda's smile merely turned sly.

"I challenge you, Grim Reaper, to a game for my soul."

"That's not how this works."

"It is now. This body is wrapped in a protection spell that you cannot pierce until you win my game."

I gripped my scythe so hard the wood groaned. Bloody humans and their *bloody* magic! Resourceful souls were always digging up despicably useful spells just to complicate my job. I glared, putting fire in my eye sockets.

"Fine. But be warned, I've made a lifetime study of chess, and I've been alive far longer than you can imagine." Every chess master in history felt obliged to challenge me. None ever won.

Brenda slid off her hospital bed. "I don't know the first thing about chess. Dreadfully complicated game. My game is much easier. A child's game: twenty questions."

I cocked an eyebrow. Well, I shifted a bony ridge on my skull. "I ask twenty questions and your soul transitions?"

"Not quite." Brenda grabbed her rolling catheter stand, shuffled to a cabinet, and bent down to rifle through it. Her hospital gown split and revealed a saggy backside. "I ask you a question, and *you* have to find the answer by asking me no more than twenty yes or no questions in return."

I scratched my jaw. "Why answer truthfully? Your soul's fate rests upon this game, you could easily obfuscate."

Brenda pulled a bundle of clothes from the cabinet and eyed them disdainfully. "There is no magic stronger than the truth. The entire spell is based on that fact. If I lie to you, the spell is broken. Turn around please." When I did not turn, she said, "I'm sure you've seen all kinds of things as the Grim Reaper, but a woman deserves a bit of privacy." Brenda made a spinning motion with her finger, white brows raised.

I faced the wall, feeling silly. There was a rustle of clothing and a few grunts before she said, "Right, time to blow this joint." I turned back to find Brenda in a heavy gray sweater, baggy slacks, and sneakers. Her catheter tube lay upon the linoleum, an orangish liquid spilling from it.

I drummed bony fingers on my scythe. Twenty questions. How hard could it be? "Very well. Ask your question."

Brenda eyed me but did not meet my gaze. The amused twinkle faded from her sharp blue eyes. "What am I?"

I spluttered. "What kind of a question is *that*? There are any number of correct answers. You are a woman, a mother, a grandmother—"

"Not a granny ... not yet," she interrupted, tugging at the sweater, seemingly unhappy with its fit. She stopped fingering the collar with a huff. "Fine, I'll narrow it down. What I am pertains to why you cannot reap my soul."

"You're a witch!"

"Sorry, was that a question?"

My teeth ground together. "Are you a witch?"

She smiled. "I clearly have magical knowledge, but no, not a witch."

"A demon? Angel?"

"No and no, though my poor departed husband thought me both at different points of our marriage." She cocked her head. "We really must be going. Do keep up." Brenda opened the door and strode out, leaving me speechless. Who was this woman?

No, that was not the pertinent question. *What* was she? I had seventeen questions remaining to figure that out.

***

The nurse's station sat frozen in time. Oops. I freeze time whenever I reap a soul to provide an opportunity for confession. In my frustration with Brenda, I'd forgotten to restart it. Two young men in scrubs leaned over a counter in mid-conversation with a young woman sitting behind a computer. I placed my left hand on my scythe below my right one, but Brenda raised her hand.

"Not yet. This'll be easier if I just disappear from the hospital." Both of my bony eye ridges rose in shock. She knew how I stopped time?

Despite a distinct hobble to her gait, Brenda was through the exit door before I recovered. I twisted the scythe viciously and time snapped into motion. Alarms sounded from Brenda's room. The young men dashed inside, then yelled at finding their patient gone. None of them, of course, saw me.

I stomped after Brenda. I could have floated, but my mood required a good stomp. I passed through the exit door and looked down. She was already two levels below me, headed for the ground floor. I drifted down through the stairwell until I was beside her again. Brenda glanced at me but didn't break stride. She burst through the ground-floor exit and hurried with that old-lady hobble through the hospital's main entryway.

Nobody glanced twice at her, just another elderly patient on her way home. I was invisible, a spirit that none see until their appointed time. One man glanced my way, an obese gentleman with wheezing breath. His eyes bulged. I pointed my scythe at him.

"I'm busy right now, but I'll return shortly. Be ready."

His wheezing breath caught, and he dropped into a chair. I hurried after Brenda.

Once outside, she stopped and glanced around. Thin arms folded across her chest as a chill Chicago wind blew through the canyon of high-rise buildings. The wind didn't touch me; I wouldn't let it. I was about to ask my next question when Brenda turned left and sped off down the sidewalk, weaving around residents headed to work.

"What's the hurry?" I said, matching her stride. "Late for an appointment?"

"No," she said without slowing. "And that's your fourth question."

"What? That doesn't count!"

"It was a yes or no question, and those count." She paused at a main street, glanced left, then hurried to a queue waiting at a bus stop.

"That's not fair!"

"I told you, it's a simple game. Simple rules. Sixteen questions remaining."

A bus pulled up with the squeal of abused brakes. Brenda climbed aboard and sat in the second row. I joined her, my teeth grinding together. The bus rumbled into traffic.

Okay, play the game. What is she? She's a saucy elderly pain in my ... no, that wasn't helpful. Dealing with her was a nightmare, but I needed to think logically...

Wait, nightmares. The sixth level of Hell is entirely populated by nightmares, horrifying figments of the human imagination made real for the purpose of tormenting souls. They rarely escape Hell, but...

"Are you a nightmare?"

Brenda's eyebrows rose. "No. Do you know many living nightmares?"

"More than you'd expect. They're really quite friendly when they're off the clock."

I wracked my brain for ideas as we rumbled down the broad avenue. After several stops, Brenda disembarked and strode into a bank. I followed, feeling like a lost puppy. Death should not be beholden to anyone, least of all a human.

Hold on, that was an assumption. "Are you human?"

Brenda glanced up at me. "Yes."

"Aha!" I'd won! She said Yes! And in only six questions. I gripped my scythe, ready to swing, but Brenda just strode away with blithe confidence and stopped at a service counter.

"I'd like to open my safety deposit box, please, but I've misplaced my key."

The clerk, a severe young gentleman in an impeccable suit, nodded. "Of course, ma'am. We'll need to confirm your identity for access. Would you follow me?"

Why was Brenda so confident that she wasn't about to die? I considered my questions. "Confirming that you're human just means I'm getting closer, yes?"

"Yes," Brenda said, which the clerk took as his answer and turned toward an office. Brenda smirked at me and held up seven fingers.

Damn! I'd used another question.

I paced outside the office while Brenda dealt with the clerk. Okay, she was human, in a hurry, and knew how I stopped time. The first two facts could describe anybody, but the last one was tricky. How could a human know about me? About Death?

Religions and philosophies were forever positing theories about the nature of death, and some even came close to the truth. The reality was that no man knows what lies beyond the veil of death. Every detail of the process is a secret, intentionally shrouded in mystery to inspire mankind to consider their wicked ways.

So how did Brenda know?

She and the clerk exited the office from a side door and descended into the basement. I followed, confident in my next question. The clerk preceded us into a massive vault, inserted two keys into a small door, and withdrew a box no bigger than a book. He set it on a table in the center of the vault and departed.

Brenda eyed the box, a strange tightness pulling her wrinkles downward. She was nervous?

It didn't matter. She was supposed to be dead. Time for question number eight. "Have we met before?"

"Yes," she said absently, then opened the box. "Often."

That ... was not the answer I'd expected. I was about to challenge her when she slammed her fist onto the table.

"That bitch!"

Brenda dipped shaking hands into the small metal container and withdrew a crisp piece of notepaper. Over her shoulder, I read the words scrawled in a jagged hand.

*How dare you hide this from me! Mireya has it now, as she always should have. I'll find your second hiding place and then, sister dear, it's time to be rid of you. Consider this your warning.*

The note fluttered back into the box. Brenda dropped her head and clasped the edges of the table, her knuckles turning white.

I assumed a conciliatory tone. "It would appear that your mission—whatever it is—has failed. Your time on Earth is done. Let us—"

"No!" Brenda's head shot up, fire burning in her eyes before she quickly averted them. Why did she keep doing that? "I am not beaten yet." She spun and stomped out.

The young clerk outside the vault jumped as if startled. He began a smooth, "Is there anything else..." but trailed off as Brenda stormed past him and up the stairs. I took a shortcut by passing through the floor and caught Brenda hobbling back onto the street.

"What are you looking for? What's so important that you've challenged the Grim Reaper in an effort to stave off death? And remember, you're supposed to tell the truth."

Brenda's stiff shoulders drooped a little. "Salvation," she whispered. "And forgiveness for what I must do to achieve it."

"Those are not my department. However, since you seem to have spare time on your hands, we passed a cathedral one block—"

"Not God's forgiveness, you black-hoodied idiot! My daughter's."

I stared at her, again in awe of this old woman's endless reserves of cheek. Black-hoodied idiot? Nobody used such a tone with Death! And it's a cowled cloak, not a hoodie. I forced my jaw to unclench.

"Then your solution is simple. Go to your daughter and talk to her. Confess, beg, sing kumbaya ... I don't care. Do whatever you need to do so I can send you to your final destination. I don't have time to chase around Chicago playing games!"

That set Brenda on her heels. She glanced up at me, lips pursed, arms crossed. "Then go. I'm not keeping you. Let me handle my own affairs, and you can continue reaping souls."

"It's not that simple. If I don't reap your soul, there are ... others who will notice and come for you. I have enemies amongst Hell's legions who dream of replacing me. Enemies who revel in making souls suffer."

"I'll take my chances."

"*I* won't."

"Very well, then, *What Am I?* Answer the question, break the spell, and you can do your job and be on your merry way!"

I had no answer. Brenda wheeled away and hailed a cab. When she climbed in, I had no choice but to follow.

*** 

We drove north into Chicago's suburbs. Autumn had turned the streets into a riot of orange and brown with leaves that swirled around our cab as it wove through traffic. The cab was warm, too warm despite the fall chill, and Brenda lowered her window. The wind brought a heady mix of moldering leaves and engine fumes.

I tried to work through the clues she had given me, but my mind kept returning to that empty box. What had she expected to find? Treasure? Jewels?

To my surprise, we did not stop in front of a house, but a library. I'd hoped my impassioned speech about talking to her daughter had gotten through. Clearly not.

Brenda hobbled up broad stairs and I followed her inside. She bypassed the circulation desk and headed for the back of the large open room, weaving through aisles of books. We finally turned into a narrow aisle. High shelves filled with nearly identical books boxed us in. Medical references, judging by their titles.

Brenda scanned book spines before selecting one from a high shelf that required her to stand on tiptoe. The tome was heavy enough that she nearly buckled under its weight, but she managed to ease it to the floor without dropping it.

Thin fingers flipped to the center of the book. Brenda's shoulders sagged in relief. "Thank God," she murmured, and I looked over her shoulder. A hole had been cut in the book's center, creating a rough square hiding place that contained a golden amulet on a heavy metal chain. Reverently, and with shaking fingers, Brenda retrieved her prize.

The amulet was half of a miniature statue of Akna, the Mayan goddess of fertility. Akna's head and shoulders dangled from the chain, but her lower torso was missing, broken in a jagged line.

I've made a point of studying the various gods and goddesses that popped up in humanity's long and sordid history. It makes my conversations while reaping their souls less complicated. Recognizing the amulet was easy enough, but why would Brenda search so desperately for this particular broken bauble?

"Are you a thief?" I asked, using my ninth question.

Brenda closed her eyes and clutched the broken amulet to her chest. "No."

"Then this prize is yours?"

"Yes, as it was my mother's before me, and her mother's before her. Passed down through the generations, this is the secret to—"

Brenda stopped and snorted. "Very good, Reaper. You almost made me give away the game. That's ten by my count. Halfway done. Do you feel that you're halfway to your answer?"

If I'd had lips, I would have pursed them. Instead, I rose to my full height and gazed at the chain dangling from Brenda's clutched fingers. "Do you feel that you are halfway to your goal?" I held up a hand. "No, don't answer. That was rhetorical."

Brenda smiled, granting me the point, and pulled herself to her feet. She looped the amulet about her neck and headed for the door.

***

Outside the library, Brenda turned right and led us down a leaf-strewn sidewalk alongside tightly packed townhouses. Buildings were faced in stone, wood, or plaster, with designs fanciful or plain but each clearly screamed out their resident's uniqueness from their neighbors.

I eyed Brenda. Leaves crunched under her feet. She was unique, strange, and infuriating. I was firmly committed to solving her puzzle, to winning her game, and she'd given away more than she'd realized. For one thing, her spell was very specific. Only yes and no answers counted against my twenty questions. If I could get her talking, she might short-circuit the entire thing and give it all away. I chose a topic sure to make any mother's tongue loosen.

"Tell me about your daughter. What is her name?"

A shadow of that wry smile quirked Brenda's lips. "Mireya, my little miracle."

Ah, the girl named on the note we'd found in the bank. "Miracle? How so?"

Brenda chewed her lip, then said, "Infertility runs in my family, a generational curse carried on the women's side. Mireya wasn't supposed to be born, but when she was, I couldn't imagine life without her."

Interesting. 'Wasn't supposed to be born' implied a plan for something that *was* supposed to happen. "Pardon me for being so bold, but wouldn't infertility by its very nature end your family line in short order?"

"Yes, it would." Brenda peered up at me, blue eyes half-hidden behind her white brows. "And that's number eleven."

Blast. I didn't word that correctly.

We turned onto a side street that looked identical to every other one: tightly packed townhouses with parked cars lining the street. I gestured to the amulet bouncing against Brenda's chest.

"So, you found a magical solution to your generational curse. Mayan magic dredged up from some ancient tome, I suspect. No, don't answer yet; I'm thinking out loud. You, or rather your predecessors, put the magic to use. But magic always has unintended consequences. Is that the reason behind your search for salvation and forgiveness?"

Brenda drew a deep breath at my twelfth question and slowed her shambling stride. "Yes, but not for its unintended consequences. I need forgiveness for what the magic *does*."

Again, the clear answer I needed, but couched in another mystery. How could fertility magic that created new life be a terrible *intended* consequence?

We stopped before a gray stone house with cheerful pastel trim. The house was split into three apartments, one per floor, with steep wooden stairs leading up to two second-story entrances. Brenda clutched the rail and climbed determinedly. At the top, she rang the left-hand doorbell.

A dog barked excitedly behind the other door. It was the deep booming sound of some massive hound. The neighbor's door cracked open several inches and caught on a chain. A dark-skinned woman's face appeared in the opening. Below her, the questing snout of the beast alternated sniffing and barking.

"Shush. Quiet!" she said. "Sorry about Bruno. He's still a puppy."

That was one massive puppy. Brenda put on a charming smile and asked, "Do you know where Mireya is?"

"She and Sebastian are at the hospital."

"What?" Concern sharpened Brenda's tone. "What happened? Is she okay?"

The neighbor smiled, a flash of white teeth. "She's about to be a mother. She went into labor an hour ago. You must be her Aunt Brenda."

*Aunt* Brenda?

Brenda stumbled back at the news. "I told her, no hospitals. The midwife..."

"Got called away to another birth, apparently. Sebastian panicked when the contractions intensified—new fathers are so excitable—and they headed to Northwestern Memorial. You missed them by perhaps ... twenty minutes?"

Brenda spun and tore down the steps. Wooden treads thumped and reverberated. She was halfway down when her left foot missed a tread and dropped out from under her. Her right knee buckled. Brenda tried to grab the railing but missed and tumbled downward. She hit the sidewalk with a *crack* and lay still.

It all happened so fast that there was a moment of silence before the neighbor screamed. She unchained the door and scrambled down to Brenda's side, drawing a cell phone from her pocket. The puppy bounded down the stairs behind her with an excited *whoof.* Brenda stirred and gasped in pain.

I glided downward and sat upon the third step, scythe across my knees. The neighbor yelled into her phone, begging for an ambulance, while Brenda's gaze followed me. Pain filled her eyes and she clutched at a wrist that was clearly broken. Blood matted her right temple.

Death is my business, but I do not like to see my charges suffer. Yet ending Brenda's suffering was beyond my power. She couldn't die until I finished her silly game and broke the spell, so I did the only thing I could think of to ease her pain.

I whistled to the puppy, and he trotted over. Bruno couldn't see me; only crows and cats possess a natural third eye, but his mind was easy to command. I placed an insubstantial bony hand on the beast's shoulder and whispered into Bruno's ear. He settled next to Brenda on her uninjured side and rested his head against her shoulder. It wasn't much, merely warmth and companionship, but Brenda closed her eyes and breathed a little easier.

"Thank you," she whispered.

The ambulance arrived with the whine of sirens and the flash of blue and red lights. With practiced efficiency, the paramedics bustled Brenda into the vehicle. I joined her—I am no stranger to ambulances—and we sped away.

***

At Northwestern Memorial Hospital, Brenda's presence in the emergency room produced no small amount of fuss. Doctors and administrators questioned her about her disappearance, demanding to know what she was doing wandering around the city after having just woken from a coma.

For her part, Brenda stoically endured their interrogations in silence, providing only enough answers to make them go away once she'd been bandaged. Broken wrist, two cracked ribs, and a hairline fracture on her tibia. I'd say she was lucky to be alive if magic wasn't the only thing staying my scythe. I spent my time waiting in the corner, again working through what I now knew about Brenda Agonos.

Her familiarity bothered me. She said we'd met before 'often.' How was that possible? Despite the teachings of several major religions, reincarnation was not actually real. Nobody knows where new souls come from—least of all me—but every newborn child is a unique creature, equal parts of its parents, but wholly its own. The mystery of life itself.

Could Brenda be a necromancer? But that wouldn't explain how she knew *me*. Reanimated bodies have no souls, which are my primary concern.

What about her relationship with Mireya? That, at least, I could get an answer to. I clicked the butt of my scythe on the linoleum, drawing Brenda's attention. She'd been pensive since the last doctor departed.

"You lied to me," I intoned.

Brenda shook her head. "Not once."

"You said Mireya was your daughter, yet her neighbor called you Aunt Brenda. Explain."

That insufferable smile appeared again. "You're getting warmer, and without asking another question. Well done. You may just win my little game yet. Where are we, eight questions remaining?"

"Indeed."

"Well, then, I'd best hurry." Brenda swung her legs off the table. The sling holding her right arm made her awkward, but she managed to unhook the monitor leads attached to her and stood. Akna's amulet swung around her neck, ancient gold glinting in the light.

Alarms sounded when the monitor leads dropped, and a nurse rushed in. She was a young woman with tired eyes and straight black hair cut in a bob. Nurse Chen, according to her name tag. "Lay back down!" she said.

"No." Brenda stepped forward and nearly collapsed, grabbing Nurse Chen's forearm for support. She straightened, despite the pain evident on her face, and pushed toward the door. "My daughter is giving birth right now and I *will* be there."

"You are in no condition—"

"You'd have to tie me down to stop me! So, either help me to the maternity ward or *get out of my way.*"

Nurse Chen's lips pursed. "Your stubbornness is going to kill you—"

If only it were that easy.

"—but I can't let you fall again. Wait here." She stepped outside and returned a moment later with a wheelchair. Brenda settled herself into it, and the nurse wheeled her into the hall and toward the elevator.

On the third floor, we proceeded through a dizzying array of hallways and ramps toward the maternity ward. I strode purposefully beside Brenda's wheelchair, long strides helping me think.

Mireya seemed to be the key to the mystery of Brenda Agonos. What was their relationship, and how could Brenda be both Mireya's mother and her aunt?

Wait. I had made an assumption from the moment I met her. The eyes are the window to the soul, but I'd only gotten glimpses of her eyes so far. She'd been averting her gaze. I looked sharply at her. "Are you Brenda Agonos?"

She sighed. "No."

Nurse Chen cocked her head. "Sorry?"

Brenda craned her head back. "Don't mind me, dear. Just having a conversation with the Grim Reaper." Chen's pencil-thin eyebrows shot up and her jaw clicked shut. Brenda eyed me, which was worrisome, but I bored into her gaze and read her soul.

Brenda Agonos indeed resided behind those eyes, but with no awareness of the world around her. A *second* soul also inhabited her body. Her sister, Analisa.

I reeled in shock.

"You are *Analisa* Agonos, sister of Brenda, mother of Mireya?"

"Yes." She glanced back. "Push faster, dear. Grim here is closing in on the truth. My time is short."

I wracked my brain, making connections. What were we rushing toward? She wasn't just a mother who wanted to be at her daughter's side through childbirth. Brenda—no, *Analisa*—knew she was about to die. Her body had, in fact, tried to die earlier today when I first arrived.

This was getting confusing. Separate the two souls. *Brenda* and her body almost died two hours ago. Analisa's soul was riding Brenda's body like a parasite. She was the one driving this train. But how? I needed more information, and I needed it fast.

I reached bony fingers to Nurse Chen's shoulder and gripped it. A shiver ran through her, and she glanced my way. To her credit, the nurse didn't scream when she saw me, but she leapt back, releasing the wheelchair.

Brenda, Analisa—whoever!—rolled free. Chen cursed, jumped to catch the wheelchair, and glanced at me. "Are ... are you...?"

"I am Death, the Grim Reaper, terror of men's souls," I intoned.

She drew a shuddering breath and then blew it out. "Good thing I'm not a man, then. You don't scare me. I've fought you my entire life." Chen shoved the wheelchair forward as though to keep her charge out of my reach.

"I'm not here for you," I said, keeping pace. "I just need answers. When was Brenda Agonos first admitted to this hospital and why?"

Both Chen and Analisa pursed their lips, but Chen answered. "She came in last week, catatonic after a stroke. No signs of brain activity until she walked out of here two hours ago."

That must have been when Analisa came on board. "Brenda has a sister, Analisa. What do you know of her?"

"Not much. Analisa was listed as next of kin, but according to our records she died seven months ago."

Bingo. I strode forward and stopped in front of the wheelchair. I raised an accusing finger. "Analisa Agonos, I know what you—"

Chen rolled her charge right through me.

I gaped at the empty hall, then spun after them. Analisa chortled as I caught up. "Thank you, dear, that was quite amusing."

I strode alongside the wheelchair, black cloak snapping with the intensity of my stride. If she wanted to do this on the run, so be it.

"You are a soul adrift."

"That wasn't a question, so I don't have to answer it."

"Fine! Are you a soul who has avoided the finality of the afterlife?"

"Yes, but that is a description, not a name. There's power in names, in titles. Wouldn't you agree, Grim Reaper? You have five questions remaining. Consider wisely."

The wheelchair curved up a ramp and under a sign with the word MATERNITY emblazoned in bold letters. The gray paint scheme turned bright and cheerful, and images of smiling animals graced nearly every wall.

Nurse Chen wheeled Analisa to the counter and asked after Mireya.

"She's in delivery," a nurse said. "If you'd like to wait—"

"Take me to her," Analisa demanded.

"Ma'am, I'm—"

Analisa glanced up at Chen. "Quickly, before the babe is born."

Nurse Chen nodded and turned the chair toward a set of double swinging doors. She threw a concerned glance in my direction.

What had I missed? I'd answered Analisa's riddle, but that wasn't enough. What was Analisa Agonos? Again, Mireya was the key.

No, not Mireya. The *babe* was the key. A new baby born to a family with generational infertility using Mayan magic to...

Fresh shock stopped me in my tracks. No, they wouldn't. Couldn't! Reincarnation was impossible. The soul cannot travel from one body to another.

And yet, rolling before me was evidence that I was wrong. Terribly wrong. What had they done? What happened to the innocent souls they displaced? A shiver ran through me.

Screams of labor pierced the hallway as Nurse Chen stopped outside a delivery room. Analisa pulled herself upright, and I threw myself between her and the open door.

"Stop, you cannot do this."

Those piercing blue eyes bored into me. Analisa's jaw clenched. "You figured out what I am."

"Analisa Agonos, are you a Priestess of Akna, Mayan goddess of fertility?"

A shiver ran through her. "Yes." Her voice was low but not defeated.

"Have you been reborn countless times using this cursed amulet?" I jabbed a finger at the glittering gold.

"Yes."

"And if I reap your soul right now, will you enter the innocent child being born?"

"Yes!"

"That was your plan all along, wasn't it?"

"Yes, and that's twenty. My protection spell is broken." Analisa spread her hands. "Do your worst, Reaper."

I clutched my scythe. "Wrong, that was nineteen. The last question is the most important. Do you love your daughter?"

Analisa's gaze snapped to the open doorway. Mireya clutched a man's hand—Sebastian I assumed—and a doctor hunched between her knees. Upon Mireya's chest lay the other half of Analisa's amulet. Analisa's confidence wavered as her daughter cried out and the doctor yelled for her to push.

"Yes," she said.

"What will happen to the child's soul?" I asked, truly curious. It bothered me greatly to think that innocent souls had been disappearing for centuries without my knowledge, displaced by this selfish priestess.

"I ... I don't know—"

Damn.

"—but this is my salvation. The Sisterhood of Akna has survived for centuries by passing our souls forward, each to their grandchild. Brenda and I are the last."

"What happened to the others of your Sisterhood?"

"Time takes its toll. Accidents, heart attacks, diseases that struck when we were unprepared."

"But then you had Mireya. An unplanned child who didn't receive an ancestor's soul."

"My mother would have inhabited her, but she died too soon. Car accident."

I leaned close. "I ask again: do you love your daughter?"

"Mireya is my everything," she said.

"As her daughter will be to her. Would you take away that joy? Make her raise you, knowing that you'd supplanted the new life that was supposed to light up her world?"

"She will forgive me. Eventually."

"Yes, but will you ever forgive yourself?" I placed the sharp tip of my scythe upon her breastbone. "I cannot make this choice for you. What will it be? Your survival, or your granddaughter's?"

Analisa eyed the scythe, her breath coming fast. She glanced into the delivery room and caught Mireya's gaze.

"Aunt Brenda! She's coming!"

Analisa's frail shoulders sagged. She drew a shuddering breath, then lifted the amulet from 'round her neck. "My granddaughter deserves a chance at life, like Mireya did."

I turned corporeal long enough to grasp the amulet and crush it in my grip. Gold dust sifted through my fingers to the floor. Analisa gulped but said nothing. I removed the scythe from her chest.

"Go to your daughter. Meet your granddaughter and be at peace. I will return tomorrow. There are more questions that require answers before you move on."

Tears filled Analisa's eyes, and she nodded before hobbling to Mireya's side.

I turned to go and caught Nurse Chen's gaze. The nurse had watched the entire exchange with rapt attention.

"Continue your fight against me," I said. "Life is fleeting and precious. I would not have it ended too soon."

With a twist of my scythe, I departed that place and traveled half a world away to the next soul in need of my attention.

***

I returned twenty-four hours later. Analisa sat in Mireya's recovery room, her granddaughter napping upon her shoulder. Though it was only mid-morning, Mireya lay asleep in the bed, recovering from her labor the day before. Analisa eyed me, and I stopped time with a twist of my scythe. The clock on the wall froze mid-tick.

I gestured to Mireya. "How much does she know?"

"Everything, now. Even that you're coming for me today." She snorted. "I'd never told her the truth of our family history before yesterday. Mireya didn't even know why Brenda insisted she wear the amulet. Thought it was just a family superstition."

Ah, yes. Another loose end to wrap up. I took the second amulet from Mireya's side-table and crushed it between my fingers over the rubbish bin.

"How did you inhabit Brenda's body?"

Analisa snorted. "Brenda murdered me when we learned that Mireya was pregnant with only one child. The amulets were supposed to give Mireya and Sebastian twins—as Brenda and I had been—but something went wrong, and Brenda wanted her reincarnation. After I died, I found myself in the most boring waiting room imaginable. Turns out that Purgatory is real."

"You'd never crossed over after your previous deaths?"

"No. None of us did. We just inhabited our newborn granddaughters. I had no idea there was anything after this life."

"How did you return?"

She smiled. "I have to keep some secrets. Suffice to say, the spirits running Purgatory are bureaucratic buffoons. It took a while, but I found a loophole."

"You seem adept at finding those."

"Hmm, yes. I came to exact revenge on my sister but found her comatose and near death after having a stroke. So, I took up residence. Better a dying body than no body. You arrived minutes after I did—bad timing there—but you want to know something funny?"

I nodded.

"Brenda was paranoid of dying too soon and always kept her protection spell active. But it was only strong enough to last five minutes after her death. Long enough to thwart you initially, but that's all. Everything else was delaying tactics until Karina was born." Analisa pressed her cheek to the baby's shock of dark hair.

My jaw dropped a little. "The entire game ... was a con?"

"And a con is the best game ever. Oh, don't be mad. We both won, though you convinced me not to reincarnate. I delayed death until *my* chosen moment while *you* won twenty questions."

I clicked my jaw shut and fought down a chuckle. Well-played. "Analisa Agonos, you were the first to win a game against the Grim Reaper, and for that I granted you an extra day. It is now time to face your future."

Analisa nodded and leaned forward to set Karina in a bedside bassinet. Then she sat back, eyes fixed upon her granddaughter.

I swung my scythe. Two souls leapt free: Analisa and Brenda. Awareness filled Brenda's eyes, and she glanced at Analisa's soul in surprise. But before she could ask questions, they faded into the ether. I didn't know their final destinations (judgements are not my department), but I suspected that Analisa would find her way back up here. I would see her again. I looked forward to the challenge.

The next soul in need of transition tugged at me, and I realized that it was the man I'd passed in the lobby the day before. I'd completely forgotten about him. Well, no time like the present.

I twisted my scythe.

*I'd like to think that Death is often challenged to games for peoples' souls, and that he's very good at the old games (like chess), but absolute rubbish at children's games.*

*It's the simple things in life that are often the hardest.*

*Analisa Agonos is another one of those characters who waltzed onto the page and made the story her own. I genuinely didn't know the answer to this absurd septuagenarian's riddle for over half the story. What was she? A right pain my scythe, for sure!*

*I wouldn't have it any other way.*

*"The Grim Reaper's Game" first appeared in the Aurora Award nominated anthology* Game On! *by Zombies Need Brains (July 2023).*

*Analisa Agonos will return in Book 3 of Grimsworld:* Death and the Immortal.

You've had a taste, now dive into Book 1 of Grimsworld:

***Death and the Taxman***

https://books2read.com/deathandthetaxman

Thank you for reading *Grimsworld Tales!*

Did you know that book reviews make authors go all soft and gooey inside?

It's true. We love hearing back from readers! Long or short doesn't matter, just share your thoughts.

If you would kindly leave a review on Amazon, Goodreads, or wherever you shop for books, you will have my eternal thanks.

Join the Lost Bard's Letter at https://davidhankins.com for more (free) lighthearted stories.

# ACKNOWLEDGEMENTS

There are, as always, so many people to thank. No book comes to life without a lot of hard work, blood, sweat, tears, and the timely application of a coffee-drip IV.

First and foremost, thank you to my wife Michelle and my daughter Beatrix. You inspire me daily and put up with an inordinate amount of authorly shenanigans. Thank you for believing in me.

To the editors and judges who first published half of the stories contained in these pages, a heartfelt thank you for introducing Grim and his unlikely cast of heroes to the world.

– Jody Lynn Nye, coordinating judge at Writers of the Future, thank you for selecting the original "Death and the Taxman" as a winner among thousands of entries for *Writers of the Future Volume 39*. My writing career changed on that day.

– Alex Shvartsman at UFO Publishing, thank you adding my very first short story "Hell's Bureaucracy" to *Unidentified Funny Objects 9*. I still laugh whenever I thumb through that anthology.

– Stephen Kotowych and Tony Pi, editors of *Game On!* by Zombies Need Brains, thank you for adding "The Grim Reaper's Game" to such a star-studded anthology. It has been a true pleasure being part of the ZNB family. And special thanks to Joshua Palmatier, senior editor at ZNB, for all you do to bring fantastic stories to life.

To the Kickstarter backers who brought the other half of these stories to life, I can't thank you enough. Between the Kickstarters for *Death and the Taxman* and *Death and the Dragon*, over 300 backers blew my expectations out of the water. You turned "Rare Find! Cordelia's Apothecary Supply," "Valhalla and Cocktails," and "Light, Lies, and Last Words" into a reality. This collection would not exist without your support. For a full listing of backers, please see the acknowledgements for *Death and the Taxman* and *Death and the Dragon*.

To the Wulf Pack writers, many of whom helped craft these stories with their keen insights and critiques: you rock! Keep writing, submitting, and publishing fantastic stories.

Finally, to Brittany Rainsdon, award-winning author and all-around amazing person: thank you for diving into Grimsworld. I can't thank you enough for your story "Light, Lies, and Last Words."

If you enjoyed *Grimsworld Tales* (and if you got this far, I'll assume you did), be sure to check out the Grimsworld series, starting with the full-length novel of *Death and the Taxman.*

Until next time,

David

# ABOUT THE AUTHOR

Award-winning author David Hankins writes from the thriving cornfields of Iowa where he lives with his wife, daughter, and two dragons disguised as cats. His writing began in the oral tradition of convincing his daughter to Go To Sleep with inventive stories. That usually backfired. After years of Just One More Story, David began transcribing his midnight ramblings in an attempt to keep his storylines straight. Children are ruthless about mistakes in their fairy tales. David writes lighthearted speculative fiction because that's what he loves to read and—this is the important bit—there's not nearly enough humor in the world. He aims to change that, one story at a time. You can find him at https://davidhankins.com

www.ingramcontent.com/pod-product-compliance
Lightning Source LLC
Chambersburg PA
CBHW060436310726
48977CB00001B/208